THE OUTLAWED DEPUTY

Cassidy Yates was appointed deputy sheriff of Redemption City but such was his knack of attracting trouble that barely twenty-four hours after his appointment he had been slapped in jail! And if that wasn't bad enough, Brett McBain's outlaw gang rode into town to bust Nathaniel McBain from jail. Sheriff Wishbone is killed and the townsfolk think Cassidy responsible.

Now, having been imprisoned for the murder of his own sheriff, Cassidy must prove his innocence and the only way to do this is to infiltrate Brett's gang. He must convince Brett he's an outlaw, and persuade everybody else that he really is an honest lawman.

Could he pull off his enormous bluff or would he join Sheriff Wishbone on Boot Hill?

THE OUTLAWED DEPUTY

I.J. PARNHAM

CULBIN PRESS

First published in 2001 by Robert Hale Limited
Copyright © 2001, 2014, 2016 by I. J. Parnham
ISBN: 9798595423717

Published by Culbin Press.

ONE

"We're waiting for you, Cassidy," Bainbridge McGruder said. "What are you going to do?"

Cassidy Yates held an ace and two jacks, which with the two aces on the table gave him a strong poker hand. After playing for two hours, he could read his three opponents' worried expressions and they couldn't beat his hand.

With everything being equal, he should risk betting whatever it took to win the pot. Unfortunately, everything wasn't equal. The sallow-faced Jebediah Michigan on his left was colluding with the gaunt, balding Granville Richardson on his right.

Bainbridge McGruder, sitting opposite, was cheating all on his own. Accordingly, Bainbridge fingered his cards, moving each front card to the back, as he had done every time he'd swapped a card from his secret pack in the inside pocket of his jacket.

They were sitting at a battered circular table and the poker players were the only customers in the Wagon Wheel saloon tonight. Situated in Redemption City, the saloon was dusty and starkly furnished.

Even late in the summer and with the sun still up, the room had an airy chill that only a permanent lack of patrons could bring. Starved of entertainment, in a town lacking anything to interest a man who'd been on the trail from Monotony for six days, Cassidy had accepted Bainbridge's offer to play poker.

Despite the cheating, Cassidy still reckoned playing had been more entertaining than sitting on his own. He was up ten dollars on the evening, but with a twenty-dollar pot, the highest so far, temptation battered at him. He adjusted his red bandanna and favored Bainbridge with his most confident smile.

"I'm in, too," he said. Cassidy counted out

and threw three dollars on to the table. "Show us what you've got."

While fingering his neatly trimmed mustache, Bainbridge licked his fat lips. Then, with a flourish, he laid his cards down to a chorus of whistles from Jebediah and Granville as they examined his six, seven and jack of hearts. Bainbridge's cards, when combined with the nine and two of hearts on the table, provided a decent flush.

"That beats me," Granville said, throwing his cards down.

"And me," Jebediah said, throwing his cards on top of Granville's.

Wincing, Cassidy regarded his authentically dealt jack of hearts. Before this hand he'd considered Bainbridge to be a practiced cheat, but clearly he had overestimated his abilities. Jebediah leaned over the table to examine Bainbridge's cards, as if he could make the heart flush become a worse hand, while Granville closed his eyes. Cassidy couldn't tell if their postures meant they knew what Bainbridge had done.

"It beats me, too," Cassidy said, deciding

the pot wasn't large enough to complain about.

With a resigned wave of his hand, Cassidy threw his cards on top of the others, face down, and pushed from the table. Standing, he tinkled his profits into his pocket. Having come into the Wagon Wheel saloon down to his last five dollars, he could walk out with twelve.

Cassidy tipped his hat and turned away. He had walked halfway to the door when Bainbridge grunted.

"What's this?" he said. "You've been holding out on us."

Cassidy turned around. Bainbridge had turned over his cards and he was brandishing both jacks of hearts. He slammed them down on the table, his jowls wobbling as he threw open his mouth in mock astonishment.

Cassidy headed back. He leaned over the table and placed his face inches from Bainbridge's.

"I'm surprised you want to let everyone know what you've been doing," he said.

Leaning back in his chair, Bainbridge smirked at Jebediah and Granville in turn.

"What I've been doing is putting up with your cheating all evening. I reckon that as soon as you saw I had the real jack of hearts, you couldn't let us know what you'd done, so you threw in your cards. Luckily, I'd spotted you cheating earlier."

Cassidy stood back from the table. "You have a duplicate pack of cards in the inside pocket of your jacket."

"Are you calling me a cheat?" Bainbridge said.

"Nope, I'm calling you a bad cheat," Cassidy said.

"Prove it," Bainbridge said, baring his yellowing teeth.

Bainbridge ran his podgy hands across his jacket, smoothing the material flat to his rounded stomach. Cassidy sighed, accepting that Bainbridge was in league with Jebediah and Granville, which meant the duplicate pack had already changed hands.

"You went to a lot of trouble to try and trick me out of my last few dollars."

"Quit the lies," Granville said. "I believe Bainbridge and you're not walking out of here with my money."

"That's the way you treat strangers around these parts, is it?"

Granville sneered. "Only the type we don't like and we don't take kindly to cheats."

With a sigh, Cassidy withdrew his twelve dollars from his pocket and threw the coins on to the table.

"Will this compensate you?"

"It sure will."

Granville smirked at Jebediah and Bainbridge, presumably because Cassidy had relented so quickly. Then he moved for the money. The second Granville's scrawny hand pounced on the coins, Cassidy hit him with the back of his right hand across the cheek, the slap echoing around the saloon room and downing Granville.

With his left hand, he grabbed the table, launching it to his left to catch Jebediah in the chest. As Bainbridge staggered to his feet to avoid the spinning table, Cassidy drew his Peacemaker and with a swirl of his hand, set the barrel firmly on him. While Granville and Jebediah sprawled on the floor, Cassidy smiled.

"Now that things are a little clearer, what were you saying about cheating?"

"I said, you're a cheat," Bainbridge said.

"A twenty-dollar pot isn't worth dying for, Bainbridge. Give me the last pot and this goes no further."

Bainbridge squared his stance. "Maybe there's only a twenty-dollar pot at stake, but this is worth dying for when I won't be doing the dying."

Bainbridge's gaze flickered over Cassidy's left shoulder and behind him, the telltale click of a gun being cocked sounded. Cassidy turned around, falling to one knee to confuse his assailant, and found himself facing a gun and behind the gun, a man with a star. The man with the star pointed at Cassidy.

"The name's Wishbone, sheriff of Redemption City," he said. "Put your gun down, stranger, real slow, or die."

Although the lawman was shorter and

over ten years older than Cassidy was, Wishbone's gaze was assured. As the other card players weren't making any aggressive moves, Cassidy nodded.

He knew the routine. Keeping his movements slow, Cassidy spun his Peacemaker on his finger. With the barrel pointed at his own chest, he placed his gun on the floor and then kicked it to Wishbone.

Still moving slowly, Cassidy raised his hands to touch the brim of his Stetson. Wishbone dropped to one knee and picked up the gun, all the time keeping his .45 trained on Cassidy. Then, stepping aside, he waved at Cassidy to follow him.

"He cheated us and tried to take everything we had," Bainbridge said as Cassidy shuffled toward the batwings.

"Of course he did," Wishbone said. "Luckily I came along when I did, before he took more than just your money."

"I'm no cheat," Cassidy said as he strode by the sheriff.

Wishbone snorted and pushed him forward a few paces with the toe of his boot.

"Of course you're innocent, and after a couple of nights in the cells to cool off, we'll no longer need to worry about who was in the right."

"Aren't you going to arrest Bainbridge?"

"I didn't see him pointing no gun at anyone, because he knows my rules. Nobody threatens another man with more than their fists in my town."

As they headed outside and to the sheriff's office that was diagonally opposite the saloon, Cassidy let his head drop in resignation.

"That's fair enough, I suppose."

"So what's your name, stranger?"

Cassidy stopped outside the sheriff's office. He took his hands from his Stetson, set them on his hips and smiled.

"I'm Cassidy Yates."

Wishbone narrowed his eyes. "Where have I heard that name before?"

"I guess it was when Marshal Devine told you I was coming."

"Why would you know U.S. Marshal Jake T. Devine?"

Cassidy laughed, his voice hollow. "I know because he sent me here to be your new deputy."

* * *

Cassidy Yates stood by Sheriff Wishbone's desk and took his oath of office. Wishbone nodded with approval. Then he took hold of his arm and directed him toward the adjoining jailhouse door.

"You've just sworn me in," Cassidy said. "There's no need for that."

"There sure is," Wishbone said. "I won't let any lawman take advantage of his position to flaunt the law. Like I said, a couple of nights in the cells should help to cool you down."

"Bainbridge McGruder cheated me. You can't expect anyone to ignore that, deputy or no deputy."

Wishbone snorted, and, with a sigh, Cassidy let the sheriff lead him into the jailhouse.

"That's more like it. You'll get no favors

from me."

Wishbone unlocked the nearest cell. Gentler than he'd been before, he maneuvered Cassidy inside. The cell already had one occupant, a fair-haired young man who had his back turned to them and was snoring. With the cell door shut, Wishbone leaned on the bars and smiled.

"Bainbridge is the worst card cheat in town, perhaps in the whole of Kansas. So you get one night in the jailhouse for drawing a gun on him, and you get a second night for not spotting he was a cheating earlier."

Cassidy closed his eyes for a moment and then threw himself on to the spare cot.

"I'm obliged for the lesson," he said with a sigh.

He settled down with his hands behind his head as Wishbone whistled happily to himself and returned to the law office. The clattering of the jailhouse door made the other prisoner stir.

"Did I hear the sheriff calling you some kind of card shark?" the young man asked around a yawn.

Cassidy reckoned the prisoner wouldn't have heard all of their conversation and he decided that admitting Wishbone had just sworn him in as a lawman might lead to a frosty couple of days in here.

"I'm the kind that ends up in jail," he said, leaning back against the bars.

The young man laughed and then offered his name as Nathaniel McBain.

"I know what you mean."

"So what are you doing in here?"

With a nervous gesture, Nathaniel smoothed his jacket.

"I got into a fight in the Wagon Wheel saloon so Sheriff Wishbone gave me twenty-eight days in here to cool off."

Cassidy whistled under his breath. "That's a tough sentence. Do you live around here?"

"What's it to you?" Nathaniel snapped.

"Nothing, I'm just making conversation. We're going to be stuck in here together for a couple of days, and I don't want to sit around in silence."

Nathaniel slapped his thigh and pushed himself to his feet. He walked the six paces to the cell door and then turned to Cassidy.

"I'm sorry, I guess I'm nervous. My pa isn't going to be pleased when he finds out what I've done to end up in here."

Cassidy shrugged. "Don't fret. After he's yelled at you, I'm sure he'll soon forget everything."

Nathaniel snorted a laugh and lowered his head. "You don't know my pa. Brett McBain is the best at everything. No one crosses him, ever. He's always done the best for me and I never want to disappoint him, but he sent me on ahead as I had a job to do before he arrived. With me in here, it doesn't look as if I'm going to get it done now."

"What job was that?"

Nathaniel opened his mouth, but then shut it quickly and waved at Cassidy.

"It doesn't matter none now. What's done is done."

With this dismissive comment, Nathaniel turned away to face the wall. Presently, the young man breathed deeply, but Cassidy didn't think he'd gone to sleep. Through the barred window above their cots the light dropped to a murky glow and Cassidy contemplated his first disastrous day in Redemption City.

His limited view of the outside world only depressed him more. Although he reckoned he had no chance of sleeping just yet, as he had nothing else to occupy his mind, he lay back on his cot and dragged his Stetson over his face.

"It doesn't matter none now," he said to himself. "What's done is done."

TWO

Riding hunched and morose, ten miles out of Redemption City, Brett McBain drew the brim of his hat farther down his forehead to shield his eyes from the setting sun. He'd hoped to finish his journey before nightfall, but with his sons, Hammond and Rockwell, devoting more time to complaining than riding, they hadn't made good time. They'd been riding north-west for four days, the miles of prairie merging into an endless green dirge.

"Ah, Pa, can't we stop?" the eighteen-year-old Rockwell asked as he rode hunched over in his dirt-streaked slicker. "I'm hungry."

"You're always hungry," Brett said. "You can eat when we reach town."

At his side, Hammond, who was two years

older than his brother, rolled back and forth as if he were sleeping.

"We're never going to get there, and it's nearly dark," he said.

Brett gritted his teeth and hoped Nathaniel had secured a place to stay tonight. That hope became even more urgent when they arrived in Redemption City. The sun had already set and the stars were growing in brilliance against the darkening sky, but none of the usual bustle Brett expected to find in a town after sundown was taking place. They trotted down the main drag, passing a store, hotel, and a church, but entertainment was only noticeable by its absence.

"Where's the saloon, Pa?" Hammond asked.

For once, Brett didn't complain about his son's unwanted question, as he was wondering the same thing. His previous visit to Redemption City had been too short to notice these details, which was why he'd sent Nathaniel on ahead.

When they reached a saloon, it was half-lit

and uninviting. Brett dragged his horse across the main drag and, after securing the mount at the hitching rail, he shuffled across the boardwalk.

A worm-holed sign proclaimed this place was the Wagon Wheel saloon. While he waited for Hammond and Rockwell to secure their horses, he confirmed that the bank stood on the edge of town, just as he'd remembered it.

A smile played on Brett's lips. Then, with his two sons behind him, he strode into the saloon. The only customers were three poker players, who all turned to him and grinned. Brett had other matters on his mind so he strode straight to the bar.

He banged a fist on the chipped wooden surface until the rosy-cheeked bartender Roger Phillips shuffled in from a back room. Roger wiped his hands on his yellowing apron and beamed happily.

"Howdy, gentlemen," he said. "What do you want?"

Brett clattered a few coins down on the bar. "Get me three whiskeys."

Roger poured three full glasses. "Are you just passing through?"

Brett sipped his drink. He swilled the stinging liquid around his mouth before swallowing to wash the grit away.

"That depends. Is it always this quiet?"

"These days it is," Roger said, shaking his head sadly. "This used to be a fine town. We used to get prospectors heading west and cattle drives from the south, but not now."

"That's a shame. This seems such a promising town." Brett and the rest stood in companionable silence for a few moments. "Right now I'm looking for my youngest boy. He came here a few days ago."

"I've seen no one new in town who looked much like you, or your sons."

"He doesn't look like them much. He's fair-haired. . . ." Brett trailed off as Roger had started nodding furiously.

"That sounds like a lad who came in here a few days ago. He shot his mouth off and a lot more besides. Sheriff Wishbone arrested him."

As Brett winced, Hammond drew him

away from the bar.

"What are we going to do now?" he asked.

Brett raised a hand, silencing Hammond, and then smiled at Roger.

"We're going to enjoy our whiskeys," he said. "That's what we're going to do."

* * *

Humming happily to himself while leaning back in his chair, Sheriff Wishbone tapped a foot on his desk with his hands behind his head. When the main door thudded open, he appraised the black-clad man in the doorway.

The only color in his attire was the tied-down brown holster. The man was gaunt without a spare ounce of fat and his chiseled face and deep-set eyes spoke of past hardships.

"What can I do for you, stranger?" Wishbone asked.

"The name's Brett McBain," the man said. "You have my boy in your cells."

Aside from Cassidy, his only prisoner was

a young man, who'd been drunk three nights back and wounded another man after an argument over a woman, a rancher's only daughter.

"He shot a man. For that, he gets a month in the cells to cool off."

"Where's the man he wounded?"

"The injured man's resting up in the Wagon Wheel saloon. Doc Parson got the bullet out and he should be on his feet soon."

Brett nodded with his eyes narrowing slightly. "I'm glad to hear it. I'll be back, soon."

Wishbone waited until Brett had turned to the door.

"It won't do no good talking to the injured man. He doesn't want to press charges."

With a grunt, Brett turned around. "Then why are you holding my boy?"

Wishbone smiled. "He's still in the jail-house because *I* pressed charges, and I say he gets a month in the cells to cool off."

Brett opened his mouth, but then slammed it shut. Breathing audibly, Brett's right hand twitched.

"I guess you're right about that. How much money do you want?"

Wishbone shrugged. "How much are you offering?"

"You can have twenty dollars, for your trouble."

As if he was weighing up this offer, Wishbone tapped his chin. When he nodded, Brett strolled to his desk using an easy, rolling gait and withdrew a wad of bills from his inside pocket. He counted out twenty dollars. Wishbone waited until the cash nestled in a pile before him.

"That looks fine. I'll see you in twenty-five days."

Brett grabbed the table with both hands and leaned forward.

"I'm not paying more than the twenty dollars we agreed."

"There's no need for more. I have to feed him for a month and twenty dollars will do, unless you want me to feed him real fancy food. That'll cost more." Wishbone leaned back in his chair. "You didn't think I was accepting a bribe for Nathaniel's release, did you, because bribing a lawman is an offense and then I'd have to throw you in a cell to cool off?"

Brett picked up his bills and breathed through his nostrils.

"I didn't. So can I see him?"

Wishbone smiled. "Seeing as you asked so nicely, no."

Brett flared his eyes. Then, without further comment, he pushed back from the desk, strode to the door and stormed outside. After a few moments, Wishbone headed to the window.

Outside, Brett joined two young men and they strode across the main drag to the Wagon Wheel saloon. Wishbone chuckled to himself and then returned to his desk.

* * *

With the early morning sun high in the sky, Brett stood outside the town's bank with Hammond and Rockwell flanking him. Today would be the culmination of several weeks of planning.

Earlier this summer, Brett had been looking for an opportunity to make some easy money when fate had intervened. On the trail outside Beaver Ridge, a wagon had approached.

Six fierce-looking guards wearing dark blue jackets had flanked the wagon with rifles brandished. They had adopted a steady canter that showed no sign of stopping no matter who blocked their way.

Brett had moved off the trail. As the entourage receded into the distance, Brett had mused that such a heavily-guarded wagon must contain something worth stealing, so he turned around and followed it while maintaining an unthreatening distance.

Whenever he could, he studied the wagon and the accompanying guards. He con-firmed the wagon was a stagecoach with the top half sawed off and replaced with a metal mesh, but what lay beneath wasn't visible.

In Beaver Ridge, a few inquiries in a saloon ascertained that the wagon was operated by Templeton Forsythe. He delivered wages to the railroad and to other local businesses, along with delivering cash to banks.

He had a reputation for doing his job well. So far, he'd never been raided. This news intrigued Brett so he tracked down the wagon outside a bank. Using the reflection in a store window, Brett had watched the attentive wagon guards transfer money to an equally attentive bank guard.

Templeton's procedures appeared sound and Brett had nearly dismissed any thoughts of robbing the wagon, but chains were only as strong as their weakest link. So he just had to find Templeton's weak link.

For the next five days Brett had followed the wagon into five large towns. In each, the same efficient process of ensuring the money went to the right people took place. He was starting to get disillusioned when his perseverance paid off.

Brett found the weak link in Redemption City when Templeton unloaded the cash delivery. The town was the smallest on the run and this bank didn't have a guard. That didn't appear to concern Templeton as without fanfare, the wagon trundled out of town and headed back to Beaver Ridge.

Afterward, Brett had hung around outside town for two days. On the first day a lumber business visited the bank and on the second day a local rancher rode into town, but few others appeared to withdraw any money.

Clearly the funds deposited here were smaller than in any other town. Accordingly, the bank was the least secure, but a small and easy pay off was better than a large and difficult one, and this bank was as vulnerable as any bank Brett had ever come across.

Best of all, this situation gave him a chance to reunite his family. He had collected Rockwell, Hammond, and Nathaniel from his uncle's farm and encouraged them to participate in his plan.

They had readily agreed to join him. So after Templeton had left Beaver Ridge for his next round of deliveries, he had sent Nathaniel on ahead to ensure Templeton's next delivery was large enough to make robbing the bank worthwhile.

Sadly, Nathaniel was now in the jailhouse and he couldn't confirm Templeton had already been here. So Brett had resorted to making discreet inquiries, and although in the saloon last night he had been treated with suspicion, he had confirmed that Templeton had come and then left two days ago.

Nobody knew if he'd left a significant amount of money and Brett hadn't wanted to press the matter. So this left him with the problem of whether to act now, or to postpone his raid until after the next delivery, when he could see for himself what happened.

"Hammond, you stay outside the bank," Brett said, having decided that waiting until Templeton returned in this quiet town would only raise even more suspicion. "Make sure no one comes in. Stop them in a friendly manner, but less friendly if you need to. Understand?"

"I sure do, Pa," Hammond said. "When do

you want me to create the diversion?"

Hammond smiled and patted his jacket as he anticipated causing mayhem.

"Everything is quiet at the moment, so hopefully not at all." As Hammond grumbled to himself, Brett turned to Rockwell. "You'll come with me, but stay back, ready to act if anybody inside reacts."

Rockwell grinned. "You can trust me, Pa."

"I sure hope so," Brett said.

He strode into the bank. To his relief, his observations of the last hour proved correct, as no one was inside except for a well-dressed teller, who was identified by a sign on the desk as being Clifford Thompson.

Like most banks along the trail from Beaver Ridge, the building had a main room with an enclosed counter along the back wall, with only one, locked entrance on the left-hand side. Behind the counter was a door to a back office where Brett presumed they kept the safe.

Clifford stood behind glass, stretching from the counter to the ceiling. At the counter, Brett smiled at the stern-faced teller until he received a smile back.

"What can I do for you, sir?" Clifford asked.

"I'm Ronald Smith and I'd like to make a withdrawal," Brett said.

Behind him, Rockwell snickered. Brett gritted his teeth, but Clifford didn't react as he opened a ledger. Then he drew his Peacemaker and held the weapon below the counter. As Clifford had both hands visible and so away from any under-counter alarms or hidden guns, Brett raised the Peacemaker into Clifford's sight. Clifford flinched and then frowned.

"I'm guessing I won't need this book, after all."

Brett smiled. "If you want to live to serve more customers, close the book real slow and step back from the counter."

Clifford did as ordered. Without being asked, he sidled with his hands above his head to the doorway to his enclosed office. To Brett's nod, he opened the door and Brett strode inside.

"What do you want, Mr. Smith?"

"Open the safe, and then I'll be on my way."

Shaking his head, Clifford headed into the back office. With a nod to Rockwell, Brett followed, staying a few paces back. At the back wall, Clifford kneeled beside the safe and, with a series of quick movements, he swirled the combination lock and threw the door open. Standing back, he waved at the safe.

"Be my guest, Mr. Smith."

Brett gestured for Clifford to stand back against the wall.

"Is everything fine out there?" he called to Rockwell.

"Yeah, Pa," Rockwell called. "Nobody's showing no interest in the bank today."

Brett gathered up two empty bags from a desk and examined the safe. To his irritation, inside there was only a small pile of bills and a bulging bag. He opened the bag, finding only a few silver coins and no gold.

Irritated, he upended the bag and kicked at the cents and dimes. Then he lunged and grabbed Clifford by the neck.

"It'd appear you're holding out on me."

"Holding out on what?" Clifford gasped with his eyes boggling.

Brett squeezed and pushed upward, forcing Clifford to stand on tiptoe. With his other hand, he pressed his Peacemaker against his neck.

"We're going to get ourselves an understanding. You volunteer information and as a reward I don't shoot you. So tell me the location of your other safe."

Clifford opened and closed his mouth, but no sound other than a faint wheezing emerged. Realizing he was squeezing too hard, Brett released his grip slightly. With a squeaking cry, Clifford gasped, his throat bulging against Brett's hand.

"What other safe?"

Brett sneered and gripped his hand tightly again. Whispering each number, he counted to ten. With each count, Clifford's face turned through brighter shades of red. Brett waited until Clifford banged his fists against his arms before opening his hand.

Clifford plummeted to the floor, dragging

in long gulps of air. Standing over Clifford's prone body, Brett gave him a few seconds to ensure he wasn't going to pass out, and then tapped his boot against his leg.

"Think about your answer, assuming, that is, you don't want to bleed to death from the new holes I'm going to make in you."

"I don't know anything," Clifford said, as he rolled to his knees, still gasping for air. With a shaking hand, he clawed at his necktie, loosening his collar. "There is no other safe."

"That wasn't the answer I want."

Brett kicked Clifford in the ribs, making him fold over his boot and slide back against the wall. The pain seemed to give the teller some fighting spirit, as he shuffled around to sit on the floor and sneer at Brett.

"I don't know what you think I have in here, but all the money I have is those coins and a few bills. There's fifty dollars maximum, probably a lot less. Take that if you want, but I have no more."

Brett strode in a circle, pondering, and then loomed over Clifford. He aimed his

Peacemaker at his head and narrowed his eyes, letting Clifford know he would have no problem using the gun.

"I don't want no fifty dollars. I have it on good authority that over the next few days you'll pay the wages for the local lumbermen and other businesses. Somehow, I don't reckon fifty dollars will cover that. So where have you hidden the rest of your last cash delivery?"

Without warning, Clifford burst out laughing and then winced, holding his ribs.

"Don't make me laugh."

"Quit laughing," Brett shouted, hitting Clifford across the cheek with the back of his gun hand.

The slap resounded in the small office. As Clifford fingered his bloodied cheek, a last small chuckle escaped his lips.

"From whose good authority would you have learned that information?"

"I ask the questions. . . ." Brett trailed off.

He had sent the good authority on ahead, and Brett hadn't been able to confirm any of these details because Nathaniel was locked in a jail cell. Unable to take out his annoyance on his wayward son, Brett advanced on Clifford. With a lunge, he grabbed him by the neck and pulled him to his feet.

"Tell me, Mr. Teller, how much money will you get in the next delivery?"

"The amount we're supposed to get," Clifford said, with a gleam in his eye that showed he still found this situation amusing. "That won't be much. We're only a small bank."

"You're not giving me the answers I want."

Brett closed his hand around Clifford's neck. Clifford clawed at Brett's hand, but fingers that were used to counting bills had no impact on Brett's iron grip.

"I'll talk," Clifford gasped, making Brett relax his grip a mite. Clifford drew in a wheeze. "Templeton Forsythe will deliver another consignment of cash next Tuesday. Then it'll be a larger amount, perhaps five hundred dollars."

Brett nodded. Behind him, his son stomped into the office.

"How do we know he's telling the truth,

Pa?" Rockwell asked.

Brett grunted in irritation and instead of releasing Clifford's neck as he'd intended to before, he squeezed his fist tighter. He kept on squeezing, his heart thudding so loudly it was if the sound was in his head.

Clifford gasped and floundered, batting his fists against Brett's chest ineffectually. Brett only relented when something seemed to give and Clifford slumped in his grip. With a step back, Brett released his hand and Clifford collapsed, boneless to the floor. Irritated with his burst of anger, Brett kicked the now dead teller and then turned away.

"Look what you made me do, boy."

"I did nothing, Pa."

"That's always the problem with my sons," Brett said under his breath.

Brett gathered up the few bills from the safe, stepped over Clifford's body and locked the office door. With Rockwell hurrying along a few steps behind, he stormed to the front door.

Then, in a reflective moment of caution,

he turned the bank sign to 'Closed'. On opening the door, Hammond hurried up to him.

"How did it go, Pa?" he asked.

Brett didn't reply and waved his collected bills, judging there to be twenty-five dollars, a poor price for a man's life.

"Badly," Rockwell said. "Apparently the last delivery was smaller than usual and Nathaniel was too busy getting himself arrested to see that."

"Quit worrying about that, boy," Brett said. "We get Nathaniel. Then we leave. Then I teach him a lesson."

THREE

Sheriff Wishbone hummed to himself as he tapped a foot against his desk. When, through the inset window in the office door, Brett McBain came into view striding toward him, he drew his .45 and checked it was loaded. A few moments later Brett threw open his door.

"What do you want this morning, Mr. McBain?" Wishbone asked with a weary air.

"I'm leaving," Brett said. "I've seen no reason to stay here any longer and I've got no intention of coming back this way."

"It's your choice, Mr. McBain. Where should I tell your boy that you've gone, assuming you want him to follow on when he's cooled off in another twenty-four days?"

"If you don't mind, can I tell him where I'm going myself?"

Wishbone wondered if Brett was still rooting for a confrontation like he had been last night, but his stance was casual and today he'd asked in a reasonable manner.

"All right, but you'll speak to him through the bars."

Brett pouted. "That's unfortunate. How am I supposed to give him a good slapping through the bars?"

Wishbone laughed. He pushed himself from his chair and picked up the key to the jailhouse.

"You can visit his cell. I'll give you two minutes alone, but you'll leave your gun on my desk and you won't give my prisoner any slapping."

Brett unbuckled his gunbelt and clattered it down on Wishbone's desk.

"Two minutes will do. I hate farewells."

"I understand," Wishbone said, as he swept the belt into his top drawer.

At the entrance to the jailhouse, Brett sighed and withdrew some bills from his jacket.

"Here, take this. It's about twenty-five dollars, for my boy's keep as we talked about last night. Make sure he doesn't starve."

Wishbone nodded and slipped the bills into his jacket pocket.

"I'm obliged. I'll look after him."

When Wishbone unlocked the cell, Cassidy Yates was still asleep on his cot. Wishbone decided that last night he'd made his point and when Cassidy woke up, he'd release him. Wishbone then left Brett with his son and returned to his desk. Two minutes later, and with the jailhouse having remained silent, Brett returned, shaking his head.

"Did you warn him about that slapping to come?" Wishbone said.

Brett nodded. "Yeah. Have you got children, Sheriff?"

"Nope."

Wishbone removed Brett's gunbelt from his desk and held it out. As Brett slipped on the belt, he smiled.

"You're a wise man. When I think about the idiots I produced, I wonder why I bothered."

Brett nodded to the window and Wishbone turned. Across the main drag by the bank, two young men loitered aimlessly by their horses. Wishbone opened his mouth to offer some encouragement, but then Nathaniel sidled into the jailhouse doorway.

Wishbone went for his gun, but Brett whirled his arm and his Peacemaker nestled in his hand before the lawman could drag his .45 from its holster. Despite his irritation, Wishbone whistled.

"You're fast."

Brett grinned. "You're not bad yourself. You reacted fast enough to stop drawing your gun; that sort of thing helps to keep men alive."

"Why?" Wishbone asked, raising his voice in the hope he'd alert Cassidy to what was happening. "I'm only keeping Nathaniel here for a month. Breaking him out of jail will make him a wanted man, and now you've drawn a gun on a sheriff you'll be a wanted man, too."

Brett grinned. "It's nice to be wanted."

"This is no joke," Wishbone snapped. He slammed a fist on the desk for additional emphasis and noise. "When I catch up with you, you'll both get a whole heap longer than a month in the cells to cool off."

Brett rocked his head from side to side. "Why did you have to threaten me? I hate that."

Light flashed and what felt like a hot fist punched Wishbone in the stomach. He fell to his knees. With his teeth clenched against the pain he knew would come when his body accepted that it'd been shot, Wishbone grabbed the side of his desk.

"Come on, Pa," Nathaniel called. "Let's get going."

The room darkened rapidly. Then it appeared to spin and Wishbone found himself lying on his back beside Brett's boots. As the boots strode to the door, darkness rushed toward him.

The door slammed shut and then time passed, but he wasn't sure how long. Then two more boots trotted into view and Cassidy kneeled beside him.

"What happened?" Cassidy asked.

"I got shot," Wishbone said as everything

went black. "It's bad. Get him, Cassidy. Get Brett McBain."

* * *

While kneeling on the floor, Cassidy examined the supine Sheriff Wishbone. The blood bubbling from the corner of his mouth suggested he didn't have much longer left. As gently as he could, Cassidy ensured Wishbone was lying straight.

Then he searched for his Peacemaker. He frantically threw drawers open, but found nothing inside. So without much choice, he kneeled and unhooked Wishbone's gunbelt. The dying sheriff mumbled when he moved him.

Then, while he hurried to the door, Cassidy wrapped the belt around his hips. Outside the office people were shouting. As he reached for the door, the sallow-faced Jebediah Michigan, one of last night's poker players, dragged the door handle from his grasp making him jerk backward. Cassidy scrambled for the sheriff's .45, but before he reached it, Jebediah uttered a strident demand.

"Hold on there," he said, aiming his six-shooter at him. "Touch your gun and you'll die."

"Forget about me and stop them getting away," Cassidy said, gesturing outside. "And fetch the doctor. Sheriff Wishbone is hurt bad."

"Wishbone's been shot, but I've caught the man who shot him," Jebediah called over his shoulder while still keeping his gun on Cassidy.

Cassidy gripped the doorframe. "Stop blocking my way. They're getting away."

Jebediah narrowed his eyes and stepped back for a half-pace.

"Your accomplices have already escaped, but we'll settle for arresting you."

Granville Richardson arrived and leaned over Jebediah's shoulder. The sight of Wishbone made Granville draw his own gun and train it on Cassidy.

"It looks like we've captured a genuine outlaw all by ourselves," he declared.

"Perhaps after this we might become deputies for the next sheriff."

Cassidy noted that Wishbone was no longer breathing.

"Believe me, if I get appointed sheriff now, when I recruit deputies you'll be the last people I choose."

Granville tapped Jebediah's shoulder. "What's this cheating murderer talking about?"

Jebediah shrugged. "I've got no idea."

"While you two varmints stand around talking, they're getting away," Cassidy said as he took a pace through the door. "We need to leave."

This pronouncement made Jebediah and Granville stretch their gun hands forward, while stepping back for a short pace.

"You are going nowhere," Jebediah said, his voice high-pitched with concern.

Granville nodded. "He's right. The only place you're going is back to your cell."

Cassidy reckoned they wouldn't listen to his protestations of innocence. Worse, both men's gun hands were shaking, suggesting they were getting worried enough to fire. With as much dignity as he could preserve, Cassidy turned around and headed back to the still Wishbone.

"Stay away from him and get in a cell," Jebediah said.

"There's no need for me to wait in the jailhouse," Cassidy said. "I'll stay here until we can sort this out."

"You either go in the jailhouse voluntarily, or you go in feet first," Granville said, gesturing with his gun at the jailhouse door.

Cassidy reckoned that arguing with Jebediah and Granville would only waste time, so he strode through the door and back to his cell. He said nothing more as Granville locked him inside.

While lying on his cot, the next few minutes passed slowly making Cassidy's irritation grow. Presently, in the office people arrived and talked, their voices indistinct.

"We need to pursue Wishbone's killer," Cassidy shouted while rattling the bars. "Let me out and we'll start searching."

Aside from an indecipherable conversation next door, Cassidy received no response. Instead, shuffling sounded, presumably from someone dragging Wishbone's body outside, followed by silence as they left him to stew on his own.

Worse, he heard no hints of the townsfolk organizing a posse to go in search of Wishbone's killer. After two hours of irritated waiting, the law office door creaked open and approaching footfalls sounded. Cassidy jumped to his feet and the moment the jailhouse door opened, he gripped the bars.

"It's about time," he said. "Do you fools realize how far you can travel in two hours? We need to leave."

A well-dressed man, who he hadn't met before, introduced himself as Victor Stanton. He shuffled closer to his cell with a gun brandished and like Granville and Jebediah, his hand was shaking.

"I'm just checking that you don't need anything," he said.

Cassidy slapped the bars. "I do need

something. I need to get out of here and find Wishbone's killer."

"Only Mayor Digby has the authority to free you," Victor said, stepping back to the wall.

Cassidy sighed. "All right, get me Mayor Digby."

Victor shook his head. "He's busy. So stay quiet. Your shouting while we took Wishbone away didn't give the sheriff the dignity he deserved."

Cassidy kept his thoughts to himself and pushed himself away from the bars. He lay on his cot and leaned against the wall. As soon as his unhelpful visitor had closed the jailhouse door, Cassidy moved over to the cell door and felt the bars, finding them solid.

Kneeling down, he examined the lock. He'd been Sheriff Quincy's deputy in Monotony for two years, and Quincy had taught Cassidy well. His abiding principle was that you couldn't beat outlaws unless you understood them.

So two years ago, Quincy had also locked

him in a cell, but this time to encourage him to find a way out of his predicament. He hadn't, but once Quincy had showed him how locks worked, he had taken only a few more weeks to learn how to force the lock.

This lesson had served him well, teaching him that breaking out of a cell was the easy part of the escape. The bigger problem came after you'd escaped. Then you needed to get past whoever was on duty.

So Cassidy ensured he was always attentive, but it didn't look as if the townsfolk were adopting the same principle because, as far as he could make out, nobody was in the outside office. This meant his only problem was escaping from his cell.

With the right tools, this would be easy, but he didn't have the right tools. So he shuffled back to his cot and felt the metal frame, searching for a weak point. As none was obvious, Cassidy yanked the cot over his head and threw it at the bars.

The cot collapsed with a satisfying crash and Cassidy rummaged through the debris. On the mangled struts connecting the base to the legs he found two thin bolts. With a few tugs, he yanked them from the frame.

Having decided they were the right length and width, he hurried to the door. He slipped his hands through the bars, maneuvered one of the bolts into the keyhole and investigated inside.

The straight bolt achieved nothing, as he'd expected, but after bending the end of the bolt between two struts from his cot, he created a satisfyingly angled shape out of the last half-inch. With one eye closed and his tongue pressed against his cheek, Cassidy wedged the fashioned key into the keyhole.

Carefully, he raised the locking mechanism inside. Smiling to himself, he pulled the now opened cell door.

"Thank you, Sheriff Quincy," he said to himself.

He trotted to the jailhouse door, which had been left unlocked by the townsfolk. In the office, he located his Peacemaker in the bottom draw of Wishbone's desk and then headed to the window.

Nobody was visible outside, but he reckoned he couldn't afford the time it'd take to find someone who would hear him out, so he slipped through the door. As three horses were outside the bank, with a confident gait to avoid drawing attention to himself, he walked across the main drag.

Outside the bank, he patted his chosen horse and leaped into the saddle. As he swung the horse around, the bank door flew open and Bainbridge McGruder rushed onto the boardwalk with two other men flanking him. Cassidy could gallop away without providing an explanation, but when he returned, he still wanted these people's respect.

"I'm commandeering this horse to go after Brett McBain and his gang," he declared. "I was in the jailhouse when he killed Wishbone. I'll pick up his trail while it's fresh and see where he fled. If he hasn't holed up close by, I'll be back by nightfall. While I'm gone, organize a posse and be ready to leave at sunup tomorrow."

Bainbridge stepped forward and gestured

with his Winchester.

"We're not taking no instructions from the likes of you," he said.

"No matter what you think of me, that's what you'll do," Cassidy said. "Now if you're not going to help me, I can't wait any longer."

Cassidy swung around. Then a rifle shot sounded and the town appeared to spin in his view. The next he knew, he was lying on the ground. Grit burned his cheek while a heavy object pressed down on his legs.

Confused, he shook his head and when his senses cleared, he found that his horse lay over his right leg. The beast thrashed, but it became increasingly weak, as swathes of dark blood pooled around its flanks. A shadow passed over him.

"Like I say, you're not going nowhere," Bainbridge said.

"You shot my horse," Cassidy gasped. To him, this sin was as bad as Brett's shooting of Wishbone was.

"I did." Bainbridge sneered. "So that's another crime to add to your list, stranger."

FOUR

After Cassidy's failed attempt to escape, the townsfolk didn't leave him alone again. Once Bainbridge had locked him in his cell, a guard stood by the cell door. In the main office, at least three other people gathered and talked, their voices too low for Cassidy to hear.

As Bainbridge had locked him in the same cell as he'd escaped from, Cassidy pushed his wrecked cot into a corner and sat on the floor with his legs drawn up to his chin. Cassidy judged that three hours had passed when Jebediah and Granville arrived.

He stood up and walked to the front of the cell. The guard moved aside after his earnest vigil leaving Jebediah to face him.

"Get away from the bars before we open

your cell," Jebediah said.

"I'm not doing anything you tell me to do," Cassidy said.

"I'm sure that won't be a comfort to Clifford Thompson's family."

"Who's he?" Cassidy snapped.

"He was the town's bank teller. Your accomplices killed him and his blood should be on your conscience."

Cassidy raised a hand. "You're wrong. I'm not who you think I am."

"We'll decide that in court."

There was no court in Redemption City, nor, with Wishbone's death, a lawman. The nearest court was in Beaver Ridge, which was several days away, meaning that confirming his identity would take longer than he'd hoped.

Cassidy sighed and rubbed his unshaven chin. It was clear they didn't know he'd come here to be Wishbone's deputy and now that he'd calmed down, he had to admit that his presence close to a dying sheriff was suspicious.

Cassidy shook his head. "We can't wait

that long. We have to act now."

Granville patted Jebediah's shoulder. "That's just what we thought. Follow us and we'll sort this out."

Seeing no choice but to follow their lead, Cassidy did as Jebediah ordered and waited at the wall until he opened his cell. Then he strode through the open door making Jebediah and Granville back away.

"Put your hands on your head," Jebediah said.

Shaking his head, but not wanting to irritate them, Cassidy did as they ordered as he strode into the office where more people milled around. He avoided meeting anyone's eye. Cassidy expected the gathered people to examine Wishbone's records and confirm his identity.

Instead, Jebediah and Granville each seized an elbow and marched him through the door. Outside, they headed along the main drag. While concentrating on not stumbling, Cassidy was led into the Wagon Wheel saloon.

As soon as he shuffled through the

batwings, Cassidy stomped to a halt. Three tables had been set in front of him and behind the tables sat a row of stern faces. Surrounding the tables, at least thirty people sat on every available chair.

Lining one wall were a row of townsfolk sitting on the bar and against the opposite wall, a double-row of people stood. Cassidy didn't think any more people could be crammed into the saloon room, and from what he'd seen of the Wagon Wheel saloon last night, he doubted it had ever been so full.

The excited conversation that filled the room faded to quiet, as one by one the gathered townsfolk turned to Cassidy. Outside, another row of people moved in to press against the windows and doorway.

Cassidy tried to confidently face close to one hundred pairs of eyes in the gathering dusk gloom. Bemused at this huge audience, Cassidy stepped back for a couple of paces, but Jebediah and Granville grabbed hold of him from behind.

With one hand on each shoulder, they

half-pushed, half-dragged him into a chair set before the tables. Once sat, Cassidy shrugged the hands from his shoulders and faced straight ahead.

"What is your name?" a short, rounded man said. He sat behind the middle table and he wore a towering black hat and a tailored jacket. A prominent gold watch and chain dangled from his vest.

Cassidy's heart thudded, but as he needed to avoid this meeting getting out of control, he crossed his legs to appear unconcerned.

"More to the point, what is your name?" he said.

"I'm Mayor Digby."

Cassidy sighed, pleased despite the circumstances to be facing someone in authority.

"I'm Deputy Cassidy Yates, but you can call me Cassidy."

With his lips pursed, Digby sneered. "Why are you masquerading as a lawman?"

"It's no masquerade. Sheriff Quincy in Monotony swore me in as his deputy two years ago. I worked well for him and fulfilled all my duties. Sheriff Wishbone was looking to appoint a deputy, and after U.S. Marshal Jake Devine recommended me to him, and with Quincy's blessing, I came here. Wishbone swore me in last night."

Digby sneered. "I've heard of Devine. I've heard of Quincy. I've never heard of you."

"I repeat, my name is Cassidy Yates," he said through gritted teeth. "I'm Wishbone's deputy, which means that you could, in fact, deem me to be your acting sheriff."

Digby uttered a low, false laugh. "I don't reckon we'd be happy to endorse a killer as our sheriff."

"I'm not a killer."

With a slow shake of his head, Digby shuffled forward and planted his elbows on the table.

"So you say, but I don't know you, or know about any new deputy being due to come here. We've always been happy with Wishbone. He kept trouble away. I can't see why he'd even want another lawman to help him."

"Wishbone requested a deputy two

months ago and here I am. I'm ready to serve you, if you'll let me."

Digby leaned back in his chair and smirked. "So you're Wishbone's deputy, sworn to be his trusted assistant in all matters, are you?"

Cassidy stretched out in his chair, showing everyone that he was assured. He made eye contact with as many people as possible, although those people did so without the warmth or humanity Cassidy expected from such an apparently decent town.

Cassidy smiled. "Yes, I'm a deputy lawman."

Digby gestured over Cassidy's shoulder. "Mr. Michigan, you brought the so-called Deputy Cassidy Yates to the court, didn't you?"

"I did, sir," Jebediah announced behind Cassidy.

Digby nodded. "How concerned did he sound for the state of Wishbone's health?"

"He never asked about him, sir."

The watchers murmured unhappily. Cassidy hadn't needed to confirm his new boss was dead, but he accepted this would look bad.

"He never asked," Digby said, intoning each word. "Wishbone served us for fifteen years with an untarnished record. Then on the day he dies his new deputy doesn't even ask about his welfare."

Cassidy shook his head. "I've seen men die from gunshot wounds to the stomach before. I knew Wishbone was dead."

"Personally, I wouldn't know," Digby said, banging his fist on the table. "I've never seen anyone die before, and I don't reckon anybody here has your expertise in spotting dead men so readily."

While everyone muttered ominously, Cassidy sighed, accepting that anything he might say would only add to his problems as it would let Digby twist his words. With this in mind, he waited until the room was silent.

"Go through Wishbone's records and you're sure to find my name."

"I'm sure we will and it'll be on a list of wanted outlaws," someone at the back of the room shouted, generating a round of tittered amusement.

"Please, no more interruptions," Digby said, raising a hand. "That's a good idea, *Mr. Yates*, but seeing as how Wishbone, fine upstanding citizen that he was, had some difficulty with the written word, I doubt we'll find anything to support your claim."

"Do you mean Wishbone couldn't read or write?"

"No, he couldn't, as you ought to know, seeing as how you're his deputy, apparently."

"I'd only just arrived," Cassidy snapped, his irritation finally getting the better of him. He leaned forward in his chair. "I never had a chance to get to know Wishbone, but he seemed to be a good man, one I'd have enjoyed working for. Now let's get this meeting over with and together we can track down his killer before it gets dark and we have to wait until tomorrow."

Digby sat with a glazed expression on his face after Cassidy's outburst.

"Letting you leave town will achieve only the terrible result I'd expect if I let a killer roam freely across the countryside, inflicting who knows what on other innocent people."

"I'm a lawman," Cassidy said. "I've never done anything wrong in my life."

"I'm pleased you mentioned that point," Digby said, his voice strident and echoing in the saloon room. "We have the matter of what you did before Wishbone's death. Would you be so good as to tell me, and our good citizens, what you have achieved in your short time here."

"Nothing. I haven't had the chance."

"Nothing? You have a strange understanding of the word." Digby paused while the crowd, to Cassidy's disgust, leaned forward, eagerly awaiting his next pronouncement. "As you're unwilling to explain yourself, I should explain to everyone here that you've spent most of your time in town sitting in a cell in the jailhouse. Presumably, you were cleaning it, or perhaps you find the cots in there to your liking."

"I was in a cell temporarily," Cassidy said over a burst of laughter from the crowd. "There was a misunderstanding."

Digby leaned back in his chair and waved his hands above his head.

"Ah, another misunderstanding was it? Mr. McGruder, if you would be so kind as to address the court."

From his position halfway along the table, Bainbridge McGruder, the card-cheat from last night, drew back his chair and stood up.

"This is no court," Cassidy said before Bainbridge could speak and make the situation worse for him with a no-doubt biased version of last night's events. "You have no authority to convene one."

"I'm the mayor. I have the right to do whatever I want to in my town. Any more outbursts and I'll have you gagged."

Digby pointed at Cassidy, seemingly daring him to defy him. Unwilling to suffer the indignity of being gagged, Cassidy pursed his lips.

"Now, simple soul that I am," Digby continued, "I'd have expected a new deputy to spend his time on arriving in a new town getting to know the townsfolk. I might have expected him to discuss matters of law enforcement with his sheriff, but apparently not. Mr. McGruder, would you tell the court why Mr. Cassidy Yates was in the jailhouse."

"Gladly, sir," Bainbridge said. He strode around the tables to stand in front of Cassidy.

As Bainbridge licked his lips, Cassidy could only groan.

FIVE

Holed up in the Lazy Dog Hotel in New Hope Town, thirty miles from Redemption City, Brett fingered the empty moneybags with irritation. By now, he'd have expected to be on his way to Beaver Ridge, already on his second horse after the first had suffered from the excessive weight of these bags, but nothing had gone according to plan.

He flung a bag at Nathaniel, who lay sprawled on his bed. The bag wrapped around his face and Nathaniel floundered as he took a couple of clawing swipes to remove the bag.

"What did you do that for?" Nathaniel said.

"You'll get worse than that if we fail again." Brett pushed himself to his feet and strode to the door.

"It wasn't my fault there wasn't enough money in the bank," Nathaniel called after him.

"It wasn't, but it sure was your fault that you didn't get to find that out, and that you couldn't tell me what you saw."

Wisely Nathaniel didn't reply, while his other two sons avoided catching his eye. Brett moved on. Once outside the Lazy Dog Hotel, he strolled along to the Thirsty Cowhand, the saloon nearest to the bank.

On pushing open the batwings, he breathed in the smell of spilled whiskey and ripe sweat, while letting the tinkle of lively piano music and excited chatter wash over him. After the sullen, deadbeat Redemption City, the sounds of ordinary folks enjoying themselves cheered him.

Feeling more content already, he headed to the bar. While he waited for the bartender to reach him, he turned to the window. The bank was at least twice the size of Redemption City's bank and that meant it'd have more money, but it'd also be better guarded.

"What do you want?" the bartender asked.

"Give me whiskey," Brett said, turning to him.

He threw a dollar on the bar and leaned on an elbow to survey the milling scene around him. He projected a calm demeanor, but his thoughts whirled over past mistakes, both recent and past.

Brett had killed his first man at sixteen, in a burst of anger over a now forgotten argument. Sheriff Wishbone was his fifth. His crimes ought to have made him a marked man with a tempting price on his head, except nobody had connected the killings.

His secret was to stay calm and to blend into the background afterward. After shooting a sheriff, some men would burn a trail in a desperate attempt to put distance between himself and the body.

Everyone would be sure to notice such a man and before long, his well-drawn likeness would appear on Wanted posters. Brett reckoned that nobody would expect a guilty man to stop at the nearest town and calmly drink in a saloon.

He was pleased that he'd again adopted this policy when, from the spill of chatter surrounding him, a man mentioned Redemption City. Brett slipped along the bar to stand closer to the man.

"Anyhow, this outlaw gang roared into town shooting up everyone," a man with a beard like an untamed bush said. "They took over the bank."

"How many were there?" his colleague asked, pushing his small, rounded spectacles farther up his nose.

"There were at least ten."

Brett spluttered over his drink and then turned his unwarranted sound into a burst of coughing.

"Are you all right, stranger?" the bearded man asked.

"I was intending to go there next week," Brett said. "From what you said, it sounds like I should give the town a wide berth."

The bearded man nodded. "For now, that'd be best. Nobody knows where this gang will strike next."

"How many did you say were in this outlaw gang?"

"It might have been a dozen," the other man said.

A bald-headed man sidled along the bar. "I heard it was fifteen. They rode through town like Judgment Day itself. Sheriff Wishbone stood alone and defiant on the main drag. He faced down all fifteen, but he paid a heavy price for his bravery."

"So this outlaw gang killed a sheriff?" Brett asked.

"They sure did," the spectacled man said, nodding eagerly. "They shot him five times in front of his own law office, but luckily the townsfolk caught one of the gang. Mayor Digby is trying him and I hope he strings him up as a warning to the rest of his gang."

While each member of the group added his section to the tale to produce the definitive version of events, Brett stayed quiet and sipped his whiskey. Clearly, the captured member of the gang was the man who had been in Nathaniel's cell. Having the authorities arrest an innocent man, and possibly hang him for Brett's crime, made Brett smile, which caught the bald-headed man's attention.

"Why were you heading to Redemption City?" he asked.

Brett didn't want these men to remember an evasive stranger, so he settled for telling his usual lie, which like all the best lies contained an element of truth.

"I'm heading west searching for land to start afresh."

"I've always wanted to get myself some land, too. They say you only need to get through the first winter and everything will be fine."

"Getting through every winter is the real problem," Brett said.

Then he settled down for a couple of hours of mindless, and hopefully unmemorable, chatter. Later, when he returned to his room, his three boys were bored after a night spent in each other's company, but the liquor had reduced Brett irritation with them.

"How much longer are we staying here?" Nathaniel asked.

"It'll be a few days before the next cash delivery arrives," Brett said.

Nathaniel nodded. "Whenever it comes, stealing the money in a town close to Redemption City after a failed raid will be tricky."

"You're right, but as I've said before, every chain has a weak link." Brett pondered and his thoughts turned to the conversations he'd heard in the saloon. "Did you talk with that man you shared a cell with in the jailhouse?"

"That was Cassidy Yates and I spoke with him for a while, but of course I didn't tell him anything about our plans."

"I didn't reckon you would, but apparently the mayor thinks he was with us. He's arrested him for shooting the sheriff."

Nathaniel turned away to face the wall. From his hunched stance, Brett could tell this news so soon after the lawman's death had affected him more that it had affected Hammond and Rockwell.

"We can't accept that," Nathaniel said.

"We can," Brett said. "Now start thinking about how we can solve our tricky problem. Somewhere there's a weak link, either in Templeton Forsythe's procedures or in how this town's bank is guarded, and we just have to find it."

"You find it," Nathaniel said, getting to his feet. "I need some air, and some liquor."

Nathaniel headed to the door, his stern gait ensuring that Brett didn't try to stop him.

"Don't get into trouble," Brett called after him. "You know what happened the last time you got some liquor inside you."

Nathaniel snorted and then headed through the door.

SIX

Only when a procession of men dragged the rope tied into a noose out of the back of the saloon, did Cassidy accept they really were going through with this. Bainbridge's testimony about his first night in town had been damning.

The account of his escape and capture, when suitably augmented, had sounded bad, too. Through this nightmarish interrogation, he had assumed he'd just have to wait until the proper authorities arrived and they would resolve this problem, but Mayor Digby didn't want to wait. The sight of the noose made Cassidy's legs shake with an unbidden tremor.

"You can't do this," Cassidy said to Digby. "I'm an innocent man."

Digby snorted. "I haven't passed a verdict yet, or the sentence. The rope's only here in case you're guilty and we decide to hang you."

"This is no court, this is no trial, and you have no authority to do this."

Digby nodded. "You're right. Wishbone is the only one with authority and as you killed him, you'll have to make do with me."

"Wishbone didn't have authority to do this either. He wouldn't preside over the murder of a deputy lawman. He'd arrest the suspect and ensure he got a proper trial by a judge from Beaver Ridge. There's a right way to do things and this isn't it!"

Sneering, Digby leaned back in his chair and gestured at Cassidy's row of accusers.

"Out here we look after ourselves, and unless anyone wants to speak up for you, I find you guilty of the murder of Sheriff Wishbone."

Cassidy stood up and waved his arms above his head. "I was in a cell when Brett McBain killed him."

"Be quiet, Cassidy, I haven't finished. You

are guilty and hanging is the punishment."

Cassidy winced. "Hanging may be your verdict, but when a proper, sworn-in officer of the law arrives, he'll conduct a proper trial. When that happens, we'll clear up this mess."

Cassidy let the rest of his statement go unsaid. After resolving this situation, he would make sure that Digby would be one of the people facing a trial for mistreatment of a prisoner.

"I'm not waiting for a sworn-in, legal officer of the law," Digby said. "I intend to hang you tonight."

With that pronouncement, Jebediah's and Granville's hands slapped down on Cassidy's shoulders. They dragged him backward and shoved him down into his chair. With a twist of his shoulders to escape from his captors, Cassidy rose to his feet and stepped out of the range of the grabbing hands. When he turned around, he faced a room full of angry faces.

"The man who shot Wishbone should swing for his murder," Cassidy said. "I promise you that I won't rest until I find him, and to do that you must do this properly. Get a message to Sheriff Quincy in Monotony about what happened. He'll send someone to confirm my story."

Digby laughed. "I don't need no proof. I have the right man."

Jebediah and Granville lunged forward and grabbed Cassidy's shoulders. This time Cassidy couldn't shrug them away.

"Don't, Mayor Digby. This is madness. I'm Cassidy Yates, your deputy."

"When we locked you up before, you escaped. That doesn't sound like the actions of an innocent man. We don't want you escaping again."

"You have my word that I won't escape." As laughter echoed around the room, Cassidy raised his voice. "And I didn't kill Wishbone!"

"If you're finished your outburst, I'll complete my ruling." Digby waited until Cassidy stilled. "I also find you guilty of assisting in the murder of our bank teller, Mr. Thompson. Now take him away."

Before Cassidy could complain, Granville slapped a hand over his mouth while Jebediah pinned his hands behind his back. So held, they dragged him backward across the saloon. Cassidy kicked his heels, but he couldn't find purchase on the wooden floor.

Within moments Jebediah and Granville dragged him through the batwings and outside. The townsfolk poured out of the saloon. During the mock trial they had murmured to each other in a subdued manner, but now they delivered a growing and excited clamor of indistinct shouting.

When Cassidy reached the center of the main drag, he was drawn to a halt and a sack was thrust down over his head. Through the tight weave of the rough sack, only the outlines of his tormentors were visible.

His backward journey resumed and as he moved through town, firebrands were lit and the crowd waved them over their heads. With his vision curtailed, he felt as if a swarm of angry fireflies surrounded him.

The shouting and screaming grew louder,

the words running together into a sea of abuse. Then Granville and Jebediah stomped to a halt. Before Cassidy could gain a firm footing so that he could try to break free, they raised him from the ground and dragged him on to a horse.

Someone tied his wrists together behind the small of his back. A rough noose scraped down over the sack to rest under his chin. Then the rope rubbed his neck as someone drew the noose tighter.

He sensed that his tormentors moved away. Then, beside his ear, a new man spoke up.

"My son, at the last, is there anything you wish to say to make your peace in this world before you enter the next?" the kindly voice said. "You have that right."

"Are you a priest?" Cassidy asked with a gulp.

"I am, but we are all God's children."

"Then listen carefully. I hardly know this town or its people, but I know this is a god-fearing town. Surely you must be able to forgive anyone, anything."

"I do, my son. Sheriff Wishbone was a good friend of mine, but I have already forgiven you for your crime."

"I've committed no crime. You're killing the wrong man and when you discover what you've done, you'll never be able to forgive yourself."

"God will forgive the sinner, provided he opens his heart to Him."

"You're not listening," Cassidy said, but he sensed that the man had stepped back.

"Neither are you," the man said from some distance away, the words faint as he disappeared into the crowd. "Be at peace, my son."

"I sure won't," Cassidy said. He drew in his breath. "Rot in hell, Redemption City!"

"Not today it won't," Digby said. "Because today, we send one more of the Devil's disciples back to hell."

"You won't do that," a new voice called, cutting across the crowd's clamor and making everyone fall silent.

"What's the meaning of this outrage?" Digby blustered.

"I'm taking charge. Now step away from Cassidy Yates and keep your hands where I can see them."

With his head turned to the newcomer, Cassidy recognized Nathaniel McBain's voice. The son of the man who had really shot Wishbone was the last person Cassidy would have thought would save him, but right now he welcomed anyone acting.

With a sudden lurch, his horse cantered forward for a couple of steps. Cassidy braced himself, expecting the noose would tighten around his neck, but the pain didn't come. Instead, the noose was dragged away from his head.

"I'm sorry," Nathaniel said. "I left that a bit late."

"Waiting another five minutes would have been worse," Cassidy gasped.

He gulped twice to confirm his neck was, in fact, free of the rope. Then Nathaniel cut the rope around his wrists letting Cassidy, with a shake of his head, remove the sack. A sea of torches surrounded him and he was on the edge of town underneath an old, gnarled tree. Cassidy fingered the tender rope burn around his neck and snarled at them, making Digby step forward.

"Whoever you are, we'll not rest until you join Cassidy in swinging," he said to Nathaniel.

Nathaniel jerked up his gun and realizing he was about to shoot Digby, Cassidy lunged forward and pushed his gun aside.

"That's not the right way," Cassidy said. "A mob can do terrible things, but these are still good people."

Nathaniel frowned, while his plea for understanding only made Digby sneer. Seeing that he could gain nothing more here, he pointed ahead and Nathaniel nodded. Nathaniel swung his horse around.

With a single shot to the heavens, which made the crowd shrink away, he bolted away from the town. Cassidy rode after him at a slow pace, ensuring he moved by Digby.

"You'll not get away with this," Digby said.

"I'm not getting away with anything," Cassidy said. "I'm innocent, and I'll prove it."

Digby launched a mouthful of spit toward him, but by then Cassidy was riding away. At a gallop, he headed out of town and followed Nathaniel into the moonlit night.

SEVEN

"Slow down, Nathaniel," Cassidy said.

This time, Nathaniel relented from his frantic dash into the night.

"We have to make sure we get away," he said when Cassidy caught up with him.

Behind them, the trail now resembled a dark stream in the faint moonlight, but there was no sign of a pursuit.

"I reckon we already have." He moved closer to Nathaniel. "So what's your plan now?"

Nathaniel wiped his forehead against his sleeve. "I guess that depends on you."

Cassidy had to bring Wishbone's killer to justice, both to prove his innocence and because he was a lawman. As Cassidy owed Nathaniel his life, this duty made him frown.

"Why did you come back for me?" he asked.

Nathaniel snorted a laugh and then sighed. "To be honest, I don't rightly know."

"Whatever your reasons, I'm in your debt. Thank you."

"That's no problem so if you want to make a run for it, we should part company here. If you want to come with me, we need to run off your horse, bury your saddle and cover our change of direction. Then we'll double-up and swing around back east to head for New Hope Town where my pa's holed up."

Cassidy smiled. "New Hope Town it is."

* * *

Forty miles out of Beaver Ridge, U.S. Marshal Tom Stannard slowed his horse and turned in the saddle.

"There's definitely movement over there," Templeton Forsythe said.

Stannard narrowed his eyes and sure enough, a rider was galloping toward them while kicking up a funnel of dust. With a nod to Templeton, Stannard dropped back and set himself between the wagon and the newcomer.

While he waited, Stannard sat tall in his saddle with his long coat pushed aside to free his .45. When the rider had crested a rise, he drew back on the reins and with a prancing, snorting slide, the horse stopped beside Stannard.

"I'm looking for Marshal Stannard," the dust-coated rider said when he had his mount under control.

"You've found him," Stannard said, tipping his hat.

The rider reached back for a saddlebag and threw it to Stannard.

"I've got a message for you, Marshal."

Wasting no time, Stannard opened the bag to find an envelope. He tore it open and read the short message within.

"We've got water," he said, stuffing the letter into a pocket. "Take some before heading back to Beaver Ridge."

"I'm obliged," the dispatch rider said, his

smile gleaming across his dirt-streaked face before he moved on.

Stannard followed the dispatch rider at a more sedate pace. When he joined the wagon, he drew alongside Templeton.

"I've got some bad news for you," he said. "An outlaw gang tried to raid Redemption City's bank. They failed, but during their escape they killed Sheriff Wishbone."

Templeton winced. "Wishbone was a good man. Have they caught the killer yet?"

Stannard drew in a deep breath. "The message didn't say, but I'll find him."

"Make sure he swings, Marshal."

Stannard nodded. He had intended to leave Templeton's group when they reached New Hope Town and head off north on his next mission, but that could wait now. He needed to reach Redemption City quickly before the trail went cold.

"With bank raiders around, be careful," Stannard called, as he urged his horse to a gallop.

"I'm always careful," Templeton shouted after him.

* * *

First light was reddening the hotel window when footfalls in the corridor made Brett stir. Rockwell and Hammond were snoring, but Nathaniel still hadn't returned after storming out of the hotel last night.

Brett drew his Peacemaker and slipped off the bed on the opposite side to the door. He rested his wrists on the bedside and aimed at the door. The door creaked open, but to his relief, Nathaniel slipped inside.

Nathaniel beckoned and a man followed him in. The newcomer was familiar, although Brett couldn't recall where they'd met before.

"Don't panic, Pa," Nathaniel said, raising a hand. "This is Cassidy Yates."

Brett nodded, now recognizing Cassidy as the man who had been in Nathaniel's cell.

"I heard they were planning to string you up," Brett said.

"They tried, but your son had other ideas," Cassidy said and snorted a harsh laugh. "He saved me."

"He always was a resourceful young man," Brett said. He smiled before turning to Nathaniel. "Why did you bring him back here? We don't need to associate with a man who's suspected of killing a lawman."

"That's my fault," Cassidy said before Nathaniel could answer. He sat on the edge of Brett's bed. "I didn't want to go far. By sundown, every lawman west of Beaver Ridge will be looking for me, but nobody would expect me to hole up only thirty miles away."

As Cassidy was reacting in the same way that Brett had, he nodded.

"In that case, you have a place to hide for the next three days."

"Why for only three days?"

Brett frowned, having accidentally revealed a part of his plan.

"We're moving on in three days."

The chatter was making Rockwell and Hammond stir and, with a smile on his lips, Cassidy stretched out on Brett's bed and rested his back against the wall.

"Based on what happened back in Redemption City, I reckon I know what you're planning to do." Cassidy frowned. "If I'm right about that, I reckon you'll fail again."

"Too much thinking can be bad for you." Brett spread his hands. "So impress me."

"In a few days Templeton Forsythe will return for his next set of deliveries, but after you killed that bank teller in Redemption City, you'll struggle to get close to the bank here."

Brett flinched and then got up. He clumped across the room and dropped down into a chair.

"The teller's death was a mistake, but I'm dismissing that unfortunate incident as being a trial run. This time, when Templeton arrives in New Hope Town, I'll raid the bank when everyone least expects it – while he's unloading the cash. This time, I'll succeed."

"You won't. Templeton guards the wagon too well."

"I'm sure he does, but I have a plan." Brett

turned to Nathaniel, who nodded. "You're welcome to join us, for a cut of the profits."

Cassidy pondered before he smiled. "So what's your plan?"

Brett rubbed his chin and then shrugged. "When I've worked out all the details, I'll tell you about it."

Cassidy nodded and rested his hands behind his neck as he stretched out on the bed.

"I'm obliged for your honesty. Now, I've had a long night and I need some sleep. When I've had some rest, I'll see if I can improve upon your plan."

Cassidy poked his hat down over his eyes. Within moments, he was snoring.

EIGHT

The sun was shining down through the open window when, with a start, Cassidy awoke. Having had little sleep for the last two nights, it seemed he'd slept until late morning. He was alone so he headed to the window.

Outside, all was quiet so he settled down to pass the rest of the morning quietly. He'd been sitting for two hours when Brett returned.

"You're awake, at last," Brett said.

"I sure am," Cassidy said. "I don't often get to enjoy a soft bed."

Brett threw a package on to his bed, and Cassidy was pleased to discover it contained a hunk of bread and cheese.

"I've just heard a rumor about you," Brett

said as Cassidy wolfed down a mouthful of bread.

Brett's expression was stern, so Cassidy chewed thoughtfully and then gave a pronounced gulp.

"I don't suppose you get many deputy lawmen helping out on bank raids."

"I hadn't heard that rumor." Brett narrowed his eyes as he edged his hand toward his holster. "I had heard that after a fair trial you escaped from the jailhouse in Redemption City by picking the lock of your cell."

"That's not what happened, but relax. I wouldn't have told you about the other rumor if it were true. I told Mayor Digby I was a lawman to buy me time to escape." Cassidy snorted a rueful laugh. "I couldn't have been convincing, as he still tried to hang me."

Brett frowned. "You should tell better lies. When I first met you, you were in a cell and you don't get many lawmen on that side of the bars."

"As I said, I was desperate." Cassidy

ripped off a slice of cheese with his teeth. "I had to do something before they made inquiries and found out about my exploits elsewhere."

"What exploits?"

Cassidy flexed and rubbed his outstretched fingers together.

"I prefer to let my fingers do the talking," he said. "I need to stay holed up here, so when your boys return, I'll get them to buy me a few things. Then I'll show you what my skill is and how it'll get us what you want."

Cassidy winked and then smiled until Brett returned the smile.

"I assume that a man who can get out of a cell can also get into a bank."

"He sure can," Cassidy said and, with that, he set to work on the bread and cheese.

* * *

Three days after arriving in New Hope Town, Cassidy smoothed down the new jacket Nathaniel had bought him and strode across the main drag. The new clothes were too large for him, but they reduced the chances of anyone recognizing him from the descriptions that must already be circulating.

If he really were an outlaw, he'd have stayed holed up in the Lazy Dog Hotel, but he had a double mission to complete. He had to appear to Brett as if he were trying to rob the bank while finding a way to arrest Brett and the rest of his gang safely.

When Brett had arrived here, he had deposited twenty-five dollars in the bank and he had withdrawn a small amount each day so he had an excuse to examine the establishment from the inside. Brett's sur- reptitious observations had let him develop his plan.

On the night before Templeton arrived, Cassidy would break them into the bank. Then they would lie in wait and in the morning they would subdue the tellers. Templeton and his guards would be at their most vulnerable when they were transfer- ring cash from the wagon to the bank.

Even better, the guards wouldn't expect a

raid to come from within the bank. So while their attention was directed at looking for trouble outside, they would come out of hiding and seize the money.

With Templeton due to ride into town tomorrow, Brett claimed that he would welcome hearing a second opinion from Cassidy on the chances of them being able to spring this trap. Clearly he didn't trust him completely, as he had insisted Nathaniel accompany him. They were two stores away from the bank when Nathaniel slapped him across the chest and pointed at a notice board where there was a new addition.

"Wanted for the murder of Sheriff Wishbone" the sign said. "Name unknown, but may pose as a deputy sheriff: reward, dead or alive $500."

"Five-hundred dollars," Nathaniel gasped. He winked at Cassidy. "I'm almost tempted."

Cassidy regarded the portrait of a dark-haired and stubble-bearded man. He couldn't help but laugh at the cold, squinting eyes and the hat that had been set at a jaunty angle.

"If you are tempted, nobody would believe I'm supposed to be that man," he said. "He looks nothing like me."

Nathaniel laughed, and they moved on to the bank. Once inside, Cassidy smiled and just to be sure, he ensured his hat was perpendicular. While Nathaniel chatted with the nearest teller, Cassidy stood at the back of the bank.

Five tellers sat behind glass that had a gap at the bottom for them to conduct transactions. Beside the counter was a closed door and behind the tellers was another door, which would presumably lead to a back office and a safe.

Cassidy knew that the protection wasn't for the people and money stored here. The doors and glass were to slow down any bank raiders and give everybody else sufficient time to organize a counter-attack.

The problem Cassidy faced was a different one than a bank raider would face. He had to ensure Brett's bank raid failed, while keeping any injuries to bystanders to a minimum, and while clearing his name at the same time.

A closed door was behind the tellers, and Cassidy reckoned that the room beyond would be the best place to spring a trap. He could corner everyone in a lockable room while ensuring the innocent parties were elsewhere.

While he thought about his strategy, a bulky and travel-dirty man clad in a short, dark blue jacket arrived. The distinctive jacket was the type worn by Templeton's guards that Brett had talked about over the last few days. Without preamble, he got everyone's attention with a raised hand.

"The name's Templeton Forsythe," the man declared, confirming Cassidy's assumption. "Clear the bank."

"I've got a withdrawal to make," the man behind Nathaniel said, confronting Templeton.

"Come back in half-an-hour." Templeton set his stance confidently with one leg thrust out and his rifle butt leaning against his thigh, showing his order wasn't open to debate. "We're about to make a major deposit."

With one eye on Templeton, Nathaniel hurried across the bank to join Cassidy.

"We'd better get back to my pa," he said.

Cassidy nodded and, as they slipped out of the bank, he avoided catching Templeton's eye. Outside, none of Templeton's other guards were here yet, but he assumed they would arrive presently.

"Templeton arrived a day early," he said as they hurried back to the hotel.

"He sure did." Nathaniel shook his head in irritation. "Have you got any idea why?"

"I assume news of your father's bank raid in Redemption City has spread and it's made him edgy enough to change his plans. Brett will have to give up on raiding the wagon this time." Cassidy shrugged. "At least we'll be able to watch Templeton's delivery procedure and perhaps spot a flaw in what he does."

"You're right, but Pa is going to be annoyed," Nathaniel said with a sigh.

Cassidy nodded. "There's nothing he can

do about it. In a few minutes Templeton will have delivered the money and then he'll move on."

"That's right, and we can't organize an alternate plan for a raid in a few minutes."

With Nathaniel's apparent reluctance to pass on the bad news to Brett, they stopped outside the hotel and faced the bank. Cassidy wondered how he could secretly get a message to one of Templeton's men without Nathaniel noticing him.

If Templeton believed his story, they could then join forces to capture Brett together. Cassidy had yet to think of a way that wouldn't alert Nathaniel when hoofs clopped as Templeton's heavy wagon arrived.

This was his first sight of the wagon and the guards looked as determined as Brett had promised they were. They were dressed in identical hard-worn Levis, dark blue jackets and blue hats that they'd drawn down low.

They were all thick-set and they rode in a well-spaced, confident way that showed they owned the main drag. With rifles brandished and with much hollering, the wagon creaked to a halt outside the bank, making Cassidy smile.

Even if he couldn't get a message to Templeton, the superior man- and gun-power they faced meant Brett faced an insurmountable obstacle and he was sure to abandon any thoughts of raiding the bank while Templeton was in town. Nathaniel's raised eyebrows suggested he was of the same mind.

Neither man needed to explain what had happened when the noise made by the rattling wagon made a determined-looking Brett come running out of the hotel with his two other sons trailing along in his wake. They all regarded the developing situation outside the bank with a mixture of frowns and surly sneers.

"We'd better go back inside before they see us," Hammond said.

"He's right," Cassidy said when Brett didn't respond. "We need to lie low in the hotel until Templeton's moved on."

Brett tapped his Peacemaker and smiled. "There's no reason to hide from the likes of him. It's time to act."

"Our plan was to sneak into the bank overnight and lie in wait for him. We can't do that now."

"Then I reckon it's time for a new plan."

"We can't take this many men on," Cassidy said, aghast.

As Rockwell and Hammond sniggered, Brett set his shoulders forward, and even Nathaniel laughed as he joined in his father's display of bravado.

"It sounds to me as if you were all talk," Brett said. "It looks like you're too scared to go through with this."

Cassidy pointed at the bank. "Templeton has got twice as many guns as we have. If you try anything, we won't stand a chance."

Brett winked. "You're probably right, but we're going to try anyhow."

NINE

Sitting at the front of a cart outside Monty Havelock's general store, Cassidy faced the bank on the opposite side of the main drag. In the early afternoon, few people were about while beside him sat a hunched Rockwell, who appeared as resigned to what was about to happen as Cassidy was.

Brett had come up with a quick plan, but Cassidy didn't think it would work, as Templeton's guards were sure to foil the raid. He only needed to follow their lead and turn against Brett at the most favorable moment.

In the bank doorway, Templeton stood poised. He nodded and another guard entered the bank, presumably to check the inside was secure. As the other guards formed a defensive circle around the wagon, Nathaniel and Brett sat on their horses beside a mercantile, one hundred yards from the bank.

They leaned toward each other, talking animatedly and not showing any obvious interest in the bank. As ahead Hammond came out of an abandoned stable on another cart, Rockwell encouraged their horses to shuffle forward.

Rockwell trundled forward parallel to the side of the main drag on the opposite side to the bank, while Hammond approached them. Brett and Nathaniel moved their horses into the center of the main drag and followed them, fifty yards back.

When Hammond drew level with the wagon, he reached into the back of the cart and when he turned back, clutched in his hand was a stick of dynamite, which he hurled toward the wagon. Brett hadn't revealed this part of the plan to Cassidy and, unable to do anything other than shout a warning, he leaped to his feet.

"Dynamite," he shouted. "It's dynamite.

Run."

"Watch out!" Rockwell shouted, appearing as shocked as Cassidy was.

The dynamite hit the ground five feet away from the wagon, and fizzing and turning, it rolled beneath it and out of sight. The horses edged the guards away and two horses at the back of the wagon bucked their riders almost to the point of dislodging them.

The other guards standing on the side of the wagon threw themselves to the ground to roll away, while those on horseback galloped away. Two guards ripped off their blue jackets and threw them beneath the wagon, as they tried to smoother the fuse.

Coming out of his shock, Cassidy tried to grab the reins from Rockwell, who still kept his steady trot forward parallel to the wagon. Rockwell drew the reins away from Cassidy's clawing grasp and directed the cart toward the wagon.

"Don't," Cassidy screamed at Rockwell. "The dynamite's under the wagon."

"That's a fake stick," Rockwell said

smiling. He raised a finger and counted for a few seconds. "This is the real thing."

From the stable that Hammond had just left a blast ripped out, sending a plume of smoke rippling out through the doorway and on to the main drag. Then, with a cascading wave of collapsing wood, the building fell in.

Thankfully, the old building would have been deserted, but with the diversion sowing confusion, the raid started as Brett and Nathaniel hurried on and splayed a burst of gunfire across the wagon. Equally thankfully, all their shots missed the scurrying guards, who were still trying to locate the dynamite while pushing passersby out of the way.

Rockwell spurred his horses on, and, within seconds, the cart had halved the distance to the wagon. Ahead, Hammond leaped from his cart on to the wagon, which was now temporarily unguarded.

Deciding he'd spent enough time posing as an outlaw, Cassidy drew his Peacemaker. In a fluid motion he aimed and fired at

Hammond. With the cart bucking and his target shrouded in smoke, Cassidy's two shots hammered into the side of the wagon several feet away from Hammond, but they were close enough to make him flinch.

Hammond showed no sign that he knew Cassidy had fired, while the guards organized themselves quickly. They dragged their horses into a row across the main drag to defend the wagon from Brett's and Nathaniel's onslaught.

Gunfire tore out, while twenty yards from the wagon Cassidy steadied his Peacemaker on Hammond. Then someone cried out behind him.

"Get him, Dave," the man shouted.

A moment later a flailing arm hit Cassidy on the side of the head as his assailant, presumably Dave, jumped on to their cart. Dave took hold of his right shoulder and spun him around.

Floundering, Cassidy tried to push his assailant, a densely bearded man, away, but then Dave gained a firm arm-lock around Cassidy's neck. Cassidy threw himself to his feet, dragging Dave forward, and then jerked backward.

With a pained cry, he landed in the back of the cart with Dave underneath him. Lying on his back, Dave's stranglehold fell away. So Cassidy rolled away from him and found that when faced with the sustained gunfire from the guards, Rockwell had lurched the cart away from the wagon.

Hammond had abandoned his assault on the wagon and was running to a spare horse, while Brett and Nathaniel galloped away, their horses kicking up vast plumes of dirt behind them. As five guards peeled off to chase after them, ensuring Brett's raid failed before it could get properly underway, Cassidy checked Dave was out cold. Then he clambered into his seat beside Rockwell.

"What now?" he said.

"We head that-a-way," Rockwell said, his concerned expression suggesting he hadn't noticed that Cassidy had shot at Hammond.

They'd reached the edge of New Hope Town when two of Templeton's guards began their pursuit. Cassidy winced, reckoning that based on what they would have seen, he'd struggle to convince the guards that he wasn't an outlaw. As the guards closed on them, Cassidy nudged Rockwell.

"We've got to do something," he said. "This cart will never outrun them."

Rockwell shot him a futile look as he cracked the reins.

"Go, go, go," he shouted.

A gunshot blasted behind him. Cassidy turned and found that Brett was drawing alongside them and he had fired at the back of the cart. Dave, the man who Cassidy had knocked out back in New Hope Town, had stirred.

With the gunshot spurring him on, Dave dragged himself along the cart toward Cassidy. Another shot crashed into the side of the cart, two feet away from Dave. At his side, Rockwell noticed the man, too, so Cassidy patted him on the shoulder.

"Get ready to ditch the cart," Cassidy said. "When I give the word, get on the horses. I'll take care of him."

Rockwell nodded, so Cassidy got up and

vaulted into the back of the cart. Dave crouched down to keep out of Brett's sight. Trailing behind them, the guards weren't gaining on them, so Cassidy steadied himself.

Then he leaped at Dave and hit him squarely in the midriff with a shoulder. Dave had set himself firmly and he only slipped back for a foot before he wrapped his arms around Cassidy's back and twisted.

They both dropped to the side where they rolled twice before they crashed into the tailboard. Cassidy braced himself for the bone-crunching fall to the ground, but the tailboard held. Dave kneeled on his chest with a fist raised ready to drive it down at his unprotected head.

"Stop this," Cassidy said, but Dave still thundered his fist down at his face.

In desperation, Cassidy threw his arm up deflecting the blow, although it still thudded into his chest. Grunting with annoyance, Dave moved to wrap his hands around Cassidy's neck, but Cassidy slipped both arms between his and forced his hands away.

He grabbed Dave's right wrist. Dave clawed at him with his left hand, the fingernails brushing his cheek, but Cassidy grasped the wrist and jerked it away. They strained until Dave shifted his weight and bore down on him.

Inch by inch his hands edged toward Cassidy's neck even though Cassidy was holding his wrists. Cassidy gritted his teeth.

"Listen to me," Cassidy said, although Dave showed no sign of relenting. "You need to get a message to Templeton Forsythe. I'm a deputy sheriff. I've hooked up with this outlaw gang to try to foil their bank raids."

Dave pressed his knees deeper into Cassidy stomach and laughed, spraying spittle over Cassidy's face. Then the cart lurched, bucking both men in the air before Dave crashed down on him.

Cassidy floundered until the cart lurched again, throwing Dave aside. Cassidy rolled in the opposite direction, steadied himself and then threw himself at Dave's back. He wrapped an arm around his neck in a stranglehold and drew his head back. Then he put his mouth close to Dave's ear.

"I'm not going to hurt you," he said. "So listen to me, this time."

Dave tensed up, but then gave a sharp nod. "Go on."

"When I've finished explaining, you'll jump off the cart. Later, Templeton's guards will catch up with you and you'll tell them that I'm Deputy Cassidy Yates. I've infiltrated these bank raiders. If we get away, I'll make sure their next raid fails and we can capture them all together safely. Understand?"

Dave struggled, but on finding Cassidy had a firm grip, he relaxed.

"I understand," he said.

Still keeping his arm around Dave's neck, Cassidy got to his feet. The guards were fifty feet away and closing. The moment they had a clear view of him they snapped up their guns and hammered gunfire at him, although it all sliced into the back of the cart.

As he doubted the second volley would be as inaccurate, Cassidy pushed Dave away and the man rolled once before he fell over the side of the cart. Then Cassidy hurried along the cart and clambered into the seat to land beside Rockwell.

"Are you ready?" Cassidy said.

"I guess we haven't got no choice," Rockwell said as he cracked the reins.

Cassidy stood up and faced the right hand horse. He leaped as a spray of bullet blasted into the seat behind him. He judged his leap well and landed on the horse's back. Wheeling his arms to keep his balance, he was thrown forward to bury his face in the horse's mane.

Spitting and holding on with white-knuckled hands, he drew back. The other horse was veering away from him after Rockwell had freed the rigging. Behind them, the guards drew back as they set in for a long chase while Brett encouraged them to be cautious with a blast of gunfire over his shoulder.

Cassidy dismissed them from his thoughts and turned his attention to his latest escape. He looped a hand under the bridle and held on as he galloped on. Behind him, gunfire rattled and the guards demanded that he stop.

"It's too late for that," Cassidy said to himself. "What's done is done."

TEN

Dave Bowman opened his eyes. He wasn't sure how he'd ended up lying in the back room of the saloon and he leaned on an elbow as he tried to get up. The room appeared to swirl around him so with a groan, he fell back to the bed. His distress gathered a man's attention and he moved over to him.

"I'm Templeton Forsythe," the man said. "You're back in New Hope Town, in the Thirsty Cowhand."

"What happened?" Dave said.

"What happened was that you were a brave, responsible citizen. As you tried to stop a bank raid, I'm authorized to pay you as if you were one of my guards."

Dave rubbed his dense beard and tried to

make sense of what he'd just heard.

"I'm hardly guard material," he said.

Templeton smiled. "Maybe you're not, but you acted when you needed to."

Dave shook his head as more of the incident that had led to him lying here came back to him. He'd been heading down the boardwalk to the saloon and he'd passed by the bank. Then shots had been fired and there had been an explosion in the stable.

Faced with a desperate situation, he had sought the fastest route away from the trouble. So he'd leaped on a nearby cart, and when one of the men on the seat had confronted him, he'd tried to drag him to the ground so he could escape.

Only when the cart had trundled out of town did he realize that the cart actually contained the bank raiders. After trying to get away without them noticing his escape followed by an ineffectual tussle with one of the raiders, he'd jumped to safety. So, with embarrassment at Templeton misinterpreting his actions, Dave shrugged.

"It was nothing," he said. "If I'm all

patched up now, I ought to get going."

"Are you sure you don't want to be a retrospective guard? The pay is twenty dollars, plus five dollars for your injuries."

With the payment reaching this heady height, Dave nodded, his misgivings forgotten about. While Templeton counted out the money, Dave cast his mind back to the events on the cart and he remembered that one of the outlaws had claimed to be a lawman, despite all the evidence to the contrary. When he had the twenty-five dollars, Dave wrapped a large hand around the bills and smirked.

"How much is it worth for information about the bank raiders?"

Templeton sneered at Dave, which was something Dave had been on the receiving end of from numerous authoritative men over the years.

"You'll get nothing," Templeton snapped. "As you're now effectively one of my guards, your duties include telling me everything you know."

Dave pouted. "In that case, I don't know

nothing."

* * *

Marshal Tom Stannard lowered himself from his horse, giving him time to take in the lay of Redemption City, a town where a lawman had died recently. As soon as he stood beside his horse, a florid-faced man hurried toward him with his short legs whirling.

"Marshal, we sure are glad to see you," the man declared as he straightened his towering hat. "We just don't know what to do."

"Who might you be?" Stannard asked.

"I'm Mayor Digby, and we're a town without no proper law. Some horrible types might waylay the good folks here now. You hear terrible things."

"You sure do. I'll need to talk with everyone who saw the man who shot Sheriff Wishbone."

"That's no trouble, Marshal. I reckon we can all do that." Digby pointed at the townsfolk who were venturing outside.

"Do you mean the whole town saw him?"

"Not when he killed Wishbone, we didn't, but we sure did see him later when we caught him," Digby babbled, rubbing his hands together frantically.

"So you've caught him? The message said the outlaw was at large."

"He is now. He escaped. We didn't know how to keep the outlaw imprisoned securely. We're a law-abiding, god-fearing town. We're not cut out to deal with his type."

Stannard nodded. "I saw you'd put up a Wanted poster in New Hope Town."

"We all respected Sheriff Wishbone. The whole town pledged to support that reward."

"It sounds as Wishbone meant a lot to you. Do you know who the outlaw is?"

Digby shook his head. "Nothing that we know for sure is true. He claimed to be Wishbone's deputy, but we knew that was a lie. He ran off with Brett McBain's boy after they'd robbed the bank."

"Did you get a name?"

"He claimed to be called Cassidy Yates."

Stannard had heard this name before. He set his hands on his hips.

"Cassidy wasn't lying about his name or about who he once was," he snarled. "But if there's one thing I hate, it's a lawman who's gone bad."

* * *

Cassidy held his hands out before the flames of their small fire, but the warmth didn't cheer him. Brett's meager supplies had been in the back of the cart and that was now lying abandoned ten miles back along the trail.

They sat beside a rocky outcrop as the sun set behind the distant hills in a reddening splash of swirling clouds. Forlornly, they passed around the stale half-loaf of bread that Rockwell had found at the bottom of his saddlebag.

Although Cassidy hadn't expected to escape from Templeton's guards, they'd abandoned their pursuit a few miles out of New Hope Town. Cassidy guessed they didn't want to leave the wagon unprotected for too long.

"Well, that didn't go according to plan," Brett said with a sigh, breaking the brooding silence.

Cassidy frowned. "That's because your plan was pathetic. Charging up to the wagon a-shooting and a-hollering after Hammond destroyed the stable was doomed to fail before it'd even gotten started."

"We achieved one thing." Brett smiled and poked at the fire. "We now know that the plan doesn't work."

Cassidy threw his arms over his head and gave a short, snorting cry of irritation.

"I joined up with you because I thought we could combine our talents. I didn't expect I'd be forced to risk my life because you've gone and got yourself a loco desire to get yourself killed."

"There was nothing loco about what we did. We nearly made it, but we were unlucky."

Brett smiled at Rockwell and Hammond, making Hammond grin.

"Did we do well, Pa?" Hammond asked as Rockwell leaned forward, too.

"Yes, you did well," Brett said.

Rockwell slapped Hammond on the back and received a slap on the back in return from Hammond.

"You did not do well," Cassidy said.

Hammond turned to confront him. "Pa said I did well, so you can't say anything else."

Cassidy sighed. "Do you know how to use dynamite?"

Hammond laughed. "I can throw."

Cassidy slapped his legs in frustration. "Which shows you know nothing about using dynamite."

As Hammond glowered at him, Brett raised a hand.

"Leave him alone, Cassidy," he said. "He made sure nobody got hurt. He lit the stick in an abandoned stable and the stick he threw under the wagon wasn't dynamite."

"That isn't the point," Cassidy said. "Are you a gambling man, Hammond?"

"No," Hammond said.

"You are." Cassidy leaned toward Hammond. "Every time you throw a stick of dynamite around like that, you're taking a dozen gambles. One day you'll lose."

Hammond turned to Brett for support, and Brett nodded.

"I agree it's dangerous, but I gave him permission to use the dynamite," he said.

"Then that was another bad decision."

"Are you challenging me?" Brett snapped.

With the four outlaws adopting stern postures, Cassidy picked up an unburned branch and poked at the fire, sending sparks rippling into the star-filled sky.

"No, I guess I'm just disappointed," he said with a sigh and a lowering of his voice. "I thought that raid would set me up for life."

With Cassidy's capitulation, Rockwell drew his blanket around his shoulders while Hammond returned to facing the fire, but to Cassidy's surprise, Nathaniel piped up.

"If you're so smart, what would you have done?" he asked.

Cassidy rubbed his chin as he wondered

what plan would be doomed to fail while sounding plausible enough to succeed. He couldn't think of one and he shrugged.

"To defeat organized guards such as Templeton's men, you need superior numbers, superior planning, opportunity and luck. The only problem is, we don't have the numbers, the planning was poor, the time we chose was wrong and we had no luck."

Brett shook his head. "So like Nathaniel says, what would you have done?"

"Nothing," Cassidy said.

"Nothing doesn't seem like a plan to me."

"It is a plan when you choose to do nothing." Cassidy spread his hands as he warmed to his theme. "We needed to pick *our* time, not the time that was best for the guards, and to generate a better diversion than destroying the stable."

"I accept that. So when would have been the best time for us?"

"The best time was as we'd originally planned: when the guards were least expecting a raid."

Brett brightened. "When Templeton's guards transfer money from the wagon to the bank, they watch everyone outside in case someone tries a raid, but they don't watch the bank."

Cassidy nodded. "That was a sound plan when you came up with it, and it's still sound. Its only flaw is that Templeton arrived before we expected him to. So now we hole up and work out what his schedule is. Then, the next time he comes to New Hope Town, we'll be waiting for him."

Cassidy gave a confident smile while hoping they didn't detect that this delaying tactic would give Dave enough time to pass his message on to Templeton. Then he would have plenty of time to come up with a foolproof plan to hand these men over to justice.

"The next time will be too late," Brett said. "After that raid and with Wishbone having been shot up, Templeton will double the guards and the chance will have gone. We have to do it now or we'll never do it."

"Then it's never."

Brett shook his head. "Tomorrow, Templeton will be in Redemption City, and we'll be waiting for him."

"We can't go back to Redemption City," Cassidy said, as Rockwell and Hammond perked up, sitting straight and eager.

"Why not?" Nathaniel asked, as Brett folded his arms in triumph as his sons agreed with him.

"After your father killed Wishbone, everybody will recognize us there. We have no hope of mounting a successful raid."

"I don't reckon so. You said we should choose our moment and strike where Templeton will least expect an attack. I'm betting that place is Redemption City, tomorrow, as he'll never expect another raid so quickly."

With everyone smiling, Cassidy reckoned he had no choice but to smile, too.

"If that's the decision, who am I to argue?"

Brett leaned forward eagerly and winked. "I'm pleased, because for this to succeed, we're going to need those limber fingers of yours."

ELEVEN

On emerging from the long grass, Cassidy kept his head down and sprinted for the back of Redemption City's bank. Once there, he pressed his back against the wall and waved for Brett and the others to follow.

The half-moon was dangling above the horizon, which meant sunup was in a couple of hours. When everyone had lined up against the wall behind him, Cassidy shuffled on around the bank.

The others followed until they reached the main drag, after which Cassidy went on alone. Under the cover of the canopy over the bank door, Cassidy checked the town. There were no signs of life, although opposite the bank in the law office a solitary light burned.

The sight of the office made Cassidy sigh before he withdrew the rudimentary key he'd cut from his pocket. He slipped the key in the door lock and poked around until a telltale click sounded.

Then, with a creak, the door swung open for a few inches. Cassidy backed away and gave a short and low whistle. When the others had joined him, they slipped into the bank where Cassidy wasted no time before he picked the office door lock. Within minutes, the five men were installed behind the counter.

"I told you I'd get you inside," Cassidy said.

"You did, but that was the easy part," Brett said before he gestured at everyone to get into position and complete their agreed actions.

Nathaniel hid in the corner below the counter while Brett hunkered down in the middle. Rockwell and Hammond left the bank to create the diversion later, one that would be less dangerous than Hammond's previous attempt in New Hope Town.

Cassidy locked both doors. Then he took up his position beside Brett and everyone settled down for the long wait. As it turned out, it was two hours after sunup before footfalls sounded outside.

A man stopped outside the door and made murmured and irritated comments to himself while stamping his heels. Presently, another man approached and he stopped. A brief conversation ensued during which Cassidy learned that the second man was William Lloyd.

He was the new teller and the other man deemed him to be late. The bank door opened. When William pattered into the room while whistling under his breath, Brett urged caution with a downward wave of his hands.

For the next five minutes, William shuffled back and forth going about his business before he opened the office door. The moment he stepped through the door, Brett rose to his feet and stood before him.

"Good morning, Mr. Teller," he said with relish.

William squealed with surprise before Brett wrapped a hand over his mouth and dragged him to the floor. Brett caught Cassidy's eye and Cassidy hurried to the main door. The man William had spoken to had moved on so he locked the door.

When he returned to the office, Brett was warning William not to raise an alarm. Then he moved his hand away from his mouth.

"What do you want?" William said.

"You don't ask the questions," Brett said. "If you do what I tell you to do, you'll live. If you don't do what I tell you to do, you'll die. Understand?"

William gulped. "I don't want no trouble. I've only just started this job after someone killed the previous teller. Please don't do anything."

"You talk more sense than the previous teller did." Brett smirked until William winced, having caught the obvious inference. "Keep this up and we'll get on fine. Now stay quiet and wait."

They all returned to their former positions while the teller sat under the counter with his back to the wall. Time passed slowly and another hour drifted by without incident until someone tapped on the main door.

"What do you reckon?" Cassidy asked.

"Ignore him," Brett said.

"A whole town can't be denied access to their bank. Someone will get suspicious soon and that's sure to cause a whole mess of problems."

Brett shook his head, but this time only five minutes passed before a second customer arrived. He talked to the first man with aggrieved tones, but they both went away. Everyone in the office breathed sighs of relief.

Then silence ensued for fifteen minutes until heavy footfalls sounded outside. The footfalls stomped to a halt and someone started up a steady thumping on the door. Brett muttered under his breath and then dragged William to his feet.

"It seems like it's time for you to open up, Mr. Teller," he said. "Make sure you serve your customer quickly and then get rid of him. Don't be nervous and don't do nothing to make anyone else nervous."

William nodded frantically and scurried off. With much rattling of keys, he opened the door.

"Why are you closed?" someone asked.

"I'm sorry," William squeaked. He coughed to clear his throat. "I didn't know I was closed. I'm still getting used to things around here."

"I understand. This place must take some getting used to. Mr. Thompson served here for over ten years."

"You don't need to tell me," William said as he shuffled back to the counter.

"He never had a hint of trouble. Then we get a bank raid, in Redemption City of all places."

"You don't need to tell me that, either."

"Why were you closed?" a second voice asked as another man came into the office.

"Apparently, he forgot to open up," the first customer said.

The second customer laughed. "My oh my, we didn't used to have this sort of problem when Mr. Thompson was in charge."

"Did you know you were closed?" a third voice asked.

In the office, William and Cassidy groaned, but Brett shrugged, seemingly accepting that if they wanted to allay suspicions, they couldn't stop the customers visiting the bank and they had no choice but to wait quietly.

An hour passed with William acting in accordance with Brett's wishes by serving his customers calmly. Then loud footfalls sounded across the office.

"It's time for you to go," Templeton Forsythe demanded.

Brett was already on alert and he shuffled to the side of the office door. Cassidy scurried across the floor and stood on the other side of the door to Brett. Beyond the door, customers grumbled as they filed outside. When quiet had descended, Templeton strode to the counter.

"I don't know you," he said.

"I'm new," William said, his voice high-pitched and nervous for the first time since Brett had given him his unwelcome task.

"Bank raiders shot Mr. Thompson last week."

Templeton snorted. "They tried their luck in New Hope Town yesterday, but we soon saw them off."

"I'm pleased to hear it."

"I'm sure you are, but I still don't know you and nobody told me there'd been a change in plan. Stay there and don't move a muscle."

Templeton moved away while William stood rigidly. A few moments later the bank door creaked.

"What's the problem?" a new man said.

"Marshal, I don't recognize this here teller. He says he's new, but I don't know nothing about a change."

"Marshal?" Brett mouthed, turning to Cassidy.

Cassidy thought for a moment until he identified the voice as being Marshal Stannard's, which made him sigh with relief, suggesting Dave had passed on his message, after all. When his relaxed smile made Brett regard him oddly, he shrugged.

"Don't worry," he mouthed.

"I only got here late yesterday," Stannard said. "I've not had the chance to get to know anyone. I'll fetch the mayor and check this out."

A few minutes passed quietly, and then a new person shuffled into the bank.

"This is ridiculous," the man said, making Cassidy grit his teeth when he recognized Digby's voice. "There was no need to drag me over here to identify a bank teller."

"Except I have," Stannard said.

Digby sighed. "In that case, yes, that is Mr. Johnson. Now, can I go?"

"No," Templeton said. "Without your sheriff, I need someone to authorize the cash to be left here. I need someone who is responsible and competent. I guess you'll do."

Digby grumbled about the implied insult. Then he stomped across the room. Inside the office everyone tensed up, but Digby stayed on the other side of the counter. A few moments of uncomfortable silence followed.

Then outside the bank, trundling sounded as Templeton's wagon approached. Brett nodded to Cassidy, while behind his back Cassidy clutched his hand into a fist.

TWELVE

Outside the bank, a whispered conversation took place. Then Templeton spoke up.

"Let's get this over with," he said.

"Do you still want me?" Digby asked.

"We'll complete the transfer," Stannard said. "Then I've got plenty of questions for you about what's been happening here."

Digby sighed. "We never had no trouble like this when Wishbone was around."

Stannard didn't respond, but Digby continued grumbling to himself. Then shuffling sounded so Cassidy put an eye to the crack in the door. While Digby glowered at Stannard, Templeton stood beside the main door with a rifle rested on his thigh.

Outside, two guards jumped into the wagon and started throwing bulging bags to the ground. Two other guards picked them up and then turned to the bank.

"Get ready," Brett whispered, tapping Cassidy's arm.

"I guess the diversion should be any moment now," Cassidy said.

When the guards reached the door, Brett nodded and sure enough, the men stopped. Then they straightened up and a moment later gunfire tore out. Lead splattered along the bank wall causing Templeton to duck.

The two guards who were holding the bags went spinning around clutching holed chests and letting the bags crash to the ground. Cassidy winced in horror. Brett had told him that his sons would fire wildly to force the guards to go to ground, but Brett clearly knew this wasn't the plan as with a grunt of pleasure, he threw open the door.

Templeton must have heard him coming as he had already turned to the office and he hammered repeated lead at the door that forced Brett to slam the door shut. The teller ran into a corner where he cowered as glass showered down on them while Nathaniel raised his head above the counter before dropping down to the floor.

Gunfire rattled and not all of it was inside the bank. Brett gestured at Cassidy signifying he should get over the counter and take on Templeton, but Cassidy shook his head and gestured for Brett to take the lead.

He figured that with Templeton being in front of Brett and with him being behind, they should be able to combine forces to subdue the outlaw, but Brett stayed by the door. Cries of alarm and pain sounded and then Templeton shouted an order that was quickly cut off.

Cassidy raised his head. Templeton was standing propped up against the door jamb with a hand pressed to his bloodied chest. Slowly he slid to his knees while to his side one of his guards slumped down to land on his chest.

Cassidy swept the broken glass away from the counter and vaulted over it to reach the main office. Then he hurried to the door to find that Rockwell and Hammond's diversion had decimated Templeton's guards.

Men lay sprawled about the wagon and they were all still. Beyond the wagon Rockwell and Hammond were making their cautious way closer and their arrival gave Templeton a burst of energy.

With a grunt of pain he forced himself to his feet. He hammered out two quick shots, and Hammond and Rockwell stumbled backward with their chests bloodied. Brett made Templeton pay for his action when he scythed a shot into his side.

Templeton toppled over and this time he didn't get back up. Then, outside, one of the defenders must have survived the onslaught as repeated gunshots sliced into Brett's sons. Both men slammed down on their backs, their chests holed repeatedly.

Behind Cassidy, Brett screeched in anguish and then while making no attempt to defend himself, he hurried across the bank. Cassidy raised his gun, but Brett brushed him aside and ran outside.

He scampered on until he reached the two men's bodies where he fell to his knees. As he hunched over them, Nathaniel joined him, albeit at a more cautious pace. Nathaniel jerked to either side as he searched for the men who had shot them, but he didn't appear to locate anyone. Cassidy moved on and regarded the aftermath of the gun battle with a sorry shake of the head.

"Nathaniel, Cassidy, get the bags," Brett said, standing back from the bodies. "We're leaving."

Cassidy shook his head and raised his Peacemaker to aim it at Brett.

"I'm sorry for what's just happened, but this is where it ends," he said. "No one is going nowhere."

"Put that gun away, Cassidy," Brett said. "This just means we'll get to split the haul three ways."

"We won't. I'm not letting you walk away from here."

"Correction," Marshal Stannard called out from beside the jailhouse. "I'm not letting anyone walk away from here. All of you put your hands on your heads real slow or you'll join those other two on Boot Hill."

Cassidy smiled as he holstered his gun and

placed his hands on his head, but Brett spat on the ground.

"I thought my boys got you," he said.

Stannard shook his head. He battered dust from his clothes as he approached them.

"It takes more than two gunmen blasting a trail through Redemption City to kill me, but that doesn't matter none now. I'm taking all three of you in. So just throw your guns down, reach and then we'll head to the jailhouse."

Brett stood his ground. "It's three against one, Marshal. They don't sound like good odds to me."

Cassidy smiled. "You're wrong, Brett. It's two against two."

"Quit the whining, Cassidy," Brett said. "Whatever your problem with me is, we can sort it out together, later. Don't side with the marshal. You'll never profit from it."

Cassidy reckoned Stannard was fast enough to take Brett, but he also feared he would take Nathaniel, too, and he was the only one of Brett's family who appeared decent enough to be worth saving. More important, Nathaniel had saved his life and he still owed him.

"Marshal, you've got no reason to trust me, but let me talk to Brett," Cassidy said.

"There's no time for talking," Brett said. "We're going."

"You're going nowhere," Stannard said, stomping to a halt. "One pace in any direction from any of you and you're all dead men."

"Brett, Stannard is the meanest shot I've ever heard about," Cassidy said. "The proof of that is lying at your feet. You've just lost two sons to him and you're about to lose the last."

Brett wriggled his fingers, shuffled his feet down and hunched forward.

"I won't lose nobody," he said. "I know I'm faster."

Stannard stepped back to get a clear shot at all three of them, while Cassidy lowered his hands and hunched forward toward Nathaniel.

"No matter what happens between you

and Stannard, you will lose Nathaniel, because I intend to kill him," Cassidy said.

"I'll kill you, if you do," Brett said, as Stannard steadily edged around in a circle.

"Don't worry about me, Pa," Nathaniel said, flexing his hands. "I can take care of myself."

Nathaniel did his best to appear committed and tough. Unfortunately, from his hen-toed stance, Cassidy guessed he had never tried to pull his gun in anger in a fast draw, at least in the company of other men.

Cassidy laughed. "Yeah, just like your brothers, Rockwell and Hammond did."

"Why you. . . ." Brett snarled and swirled his hand.

Cassidy thrust his hand down, drew his Peacemaker and fired at Nathaniel, but he aimed for his hand and blasted his gun away while it was still halfway out of its holster. As two other gunshots echoed, Brett and Stannard both stood with their guns drawn, swirls of gunsmoke drifting between them.

Cassidy hunched forward ready to take Brett, but Brett's knees crumpled and then he fell backward to land with a grunt on the ground. Clutching his wounded hand, Nathaniel dashed to his father, but the rose of blood spreading across Brett's chest made him recoil.

Stannard, with a swift spin of his hand, thrust his own .45 back in his holster. He nodded to Cassidy.

"You two are now going to the jailhouse," he said.

"There's no need to lock me up, Marshal," Cassidy said.

"Am I right in thinking from that request that you're Deputy Cassidy Yates?"

"I sure am, although I prefer Cassidy, which means I'm on your side of the law."

Stannard shook his head and then gestured at the law office.

"I was sure beforehand that you'd claim that, and I expect now you'll claim you didn't kill Sheriff Wishbone or do any of the things Mayor Digby claims you're responsible for."

"I'm not guilty of anything the mayor says I've done," Cassidy snapped.

"That's as maybe, but you're guilty of everything else."

"What else? I only stayed with Brett's gang to make sure they failed, and that no one else was hurt."

Stannard pointed at the body of the nearest guard. "Then you failed. You forgot you were a lawman and this is the result."

Cassidy conceded Stannard's point with a sigh and moved on to Brett's body. He patted Nathaniel's shoulder, making Nathaniel flinch away from him.

"I've got no family now," he said.

"Let's move on," Cassidy said, reckoning that any comforting words he offered would have the opposite effect.

Nathaniel offered no complaints when he led him to the law office and then to the jailhouse. He went into a cell with his head lowered, but Cassidy stopped outside the cell that Wishbone had locked him inside only a few days ago.

"I tried to lessen the damage," he said. "I did my best."

Stannard said nothing until Cassidy

moved into the cell.

"Your best wasn't good enough. Once you're a lawman, you're always a lawman. You don't pretend to be an outlaw and hope to make things better. You betrayed the badge, and yourself."

"You're wrong," Cassidy said, gripping the bars. "I was trapped on all sides. What could I do?"

At the door, Stannard shook his head. "Die. That's what you could have done, but at least you'd have died a lawman. A lawman never abandons his duty and you did."

Stannard slammed and locked the door, and when he walked away, Cassidy turned around. Nathaniel was sitting on the cot Cassidy had wrecked the last time he had been here.

"Nathaniel, I'll make sure you don't take all the blame here," he said. "What you did will only get you a few years in jail."

"Don't speak to me," Nathaniel said and drew his legs up to his chin.

So, with a groan, Cassidy slumped down on the floor and folded his arms.

THIRTEEN

When the frosty silence in the cell dragged on Cassidy's nerves, he raised himself to the barred cell window. Some of the townsfolk were heading toward the bank while others loitered farther away.

Stannard ushered the watchers away and urged the braver ones to help him. A doctor moved around inspecting the guards' bodies and then stood back to let them be taken away into the saloon.

With this process underway, Digby arrived. To Cassidy's irritation, he stood in the bank doorway and he didn't offer to help Stannard collect the unclaimed moneybags. The marshal piled them up outside the bank and then turned to the townsfolk, presumably working out who he could trust to help him take them into the bank.

Cassidy smiled when the marshal ignored Digby, confirming that another lawman had the same view of this man as he had. Then Cassidy's heart quickened. Something was wrong here. Something had always been wrong here.

Decent, law-abiding folks shouldn't try to lynch the first man they find after a death, even when a lawman had been shot up. The mayor shouldn't argue with a U.S. marshal and whine about cash deliveries at banks.

Cassidy patted his pockets and inside his jacket was the slip of metal he'd used to break into the bank. Cassidy smiled and moved to the cell door. He reached through the bars and with a few deft movements, he managed to spring the lock letting the door swing open.

He hurried on to the jailhouse door where he stopped. The morose Nathaniel sat with his knees drawn up to his chin, lost in his own thoughts, so Cassidy slipped into the main office. He located his Peacemaker in a desk and then dashed to the door and outside where he strode toward Stannard while keeping one eye on Digby.

"Look out, Marshal," Digby said, and pointed at Cassidy. "One of your charges is trying to escape."

Cassidy holstered his gun, but he kept his posture relaxed in case Digby acted.

Stannard shook his head. "Cassidy, you aren't making this easy on yourself."

Cassidy strode on toward Stannard, only stopping when he was ten paces away from him.

"Marshal, we need to talk," he said.

"I have no interest in anything you might say. I've a task to do and I'll finish it, whereas you had your chance and you didn't take it. So wait in your cell for me to take you back to Beaver Ridge."

Cassidy backed away a pace and pointed to the moneybags lying between Digby and Stannard.

"I will, but don't forget the money," he said. "I wouldn't leave them out here. You don't know what types might seize the opportunity for a little stealing."

Stannard nodded, but Digby strode between them and raised a hand.

"I resent that insult," he said.

Digby's nervous comment only confirmed to Cassidy that he was right. With his anger bubbling over, Cassidy moved forward, grabbed Digby's shoulder and swung him around.

"Why have you never improved security here, Digby?"

Digby shook in his grasp, failing to free himself from Cassidy's strong grip of his shoulder.

"I wouldn't know," he said. "I don't concern myself in such matters."

Stannard kneeled on the ground and gathered up several bags, but then paused.

"What are you getting at, Cassidy?" he asked with an exasperated sigh.

Cassidy was about to answer, but several people had strayed outside including Bainbridge and Jebediah, along with a few others that he recognized from the town's attempt to lynch him, and they were edging closer.

"Marshal, something is wrong here," Cassidy said while backing away from Digby.

Stannard laughed. "Don't worry, Cassidy. I'll make sure you get a fair trial in Beaver Ridge. These folks won't lynch you."

"I believe you'll try, but they failed the first time," Cassidy said. "Today they'll fail again."

Stannard shrugged, his expression displaying a mixture of horror and surprise, but any hope that he'd said enough to convince the marshal fled when Cassidy realized that his comment hadn't shocked him. Nathaniel had left the jailhouse.

Nathaniel was moving on to the cart, which would now contain his father's body. Clutched in his right hand was his father's Peacemaker. The hand was bloody, but the determination in Nathaniel's eyes said the injury wouldn't stop him firing.

"Put down that gun, now," Stannard ordered. "If you don't, I'll be forced to kill you."

"Wait," Cassidy said, raising an arm. "Let

me talk to him."

Ignoring Digby, who muttered under his breath, Cassidy strode toward Nathaniel, but that made the young man turn his Peacemaker on him.

"No farther, Cassidy," Nathaniel said. "I've got nothing to lose no more."

Cassidy held his arms wide apart, making a show of moving them away from his Peacemaker.

"You've got everything to lose. You have the chance of a new life and it'll be a better life than if you shoot me."

"After what you did to my pa, all that matters is making sure you don't live."

Cassidy frowned. "I'm not responsible for what happened to Brett."

"I saw what happened," Nathaniel snarled, his eyes wild. "You and Stannard did it. I don't know which one pulled the trigger, but Stannard was only doing his duty. You're worse. I saved your life, but you turned on us, just like you always intended to do."

"Brett chose his path and he chose the wrong one for himself and for you."

"My pa did what he thought was best." Nathaniel raised his Peacemaker to sight Cassidy's head. "You can't judge him."

As Stannard settled his stance, clearly preparing to act, Cassidy sighed.

"Brett was a gunslinger and Stannard couldn't defeat him. Brett knew I wouldn't kill you so he lost deliberately. He wanted you to have a better life than living as a wanted outlaw."

Cassidy doubted that was what had happened, but he hoped it was a believable possibility.

"He didn't," Nathaniel said. He gulped and ran an arm over his sweating brow. "You defeated him."

Cassidy advanced a short pace. "Brett wasn't scared of nobody. He could outthink and outshoot himself from any situation. He'd have killed Stannard and me easily, but he didn't want you and he to be running for the rest of your lives."

Nathaniel shook his head, forcing Stannard to edge forward.

"Cassidy, step aside," Stannard said. "I'll

deal with this."

Cassidy shook his head. "You won't. Nathaniel will go back to his cell. He's a decent man with a conscience. He came back for me and saved my life. It's time for him to be that man again."

"Don't trust him, Marshal," Digby said from behind him. "They're working together."

Digby had picked up two of the money-bags, convincing Cassidy that he intended to use the distraction to sneak away with them. Cassidy drew his Peacemaker and aimed it at Digby.

"Put those bags down or I'll shoot," he said.

"Stop this," Stannard said. He drew his .45 and turned it on Cassidy.

Cassidy shook his head. "I don't know exactly what's going on here, but I reckon Brett was right. A chain *is* as strong as its weakest link, and the weak link lives in Redemption City. So put the bags down and step away from them, Digby."

Digby pointed at Nathaniel, his mouth

falling open in apparent horror.

"We're surrounded," he said. "Nathaniel's got a gun on you, and Cassidy's gun is on me. Marshal, stop them."

Stannard narrowed his eyes. "What's your point, Cassidy?"

"This bank is the worst guarded one that Templeton used to visit. That's because Digby is in charge of this town and he wants to be able to get his hands on the money whenever he wants."

Digby squealed in anguish and then dropped the bags before diving to the ground. Working on instinct, Cassidy dove to the ground, too, and a moment later gunfire from the nearest townsfolk ricocheted around him.

He scrambled over the ground to the cart followed by Stannard. Twenty paces before them, a row of townsfolk dashed for cover behind the wagon while firing wildly. In retaliation, Cassidy fired off three quick shots, catching two men with high shots to the chest before they reached cover.

With a lull, they swung behind the cart to

find Nathaniel already hunched down. Without time to check on where Nathaniel's loyalties lay, Cassidy took hold of the underside of the cart and tugged upward.

The cart was too heavy, but Stannard joined him in trying to raise it followed by Nathaniel. With much creaking, the cart toppled over and Cassidy ducked down behind the cover.

"What are we going to do, now?" he asked Stannard.

Stannard grinned and flexed his fingers. "We fight."

FOURTEEN

"You've got a choice, Nathaniel," Cassidy said, as he reloaded. "Join us or go against us. What's it to be?"

Nathaniel smiled. "The way I see it, either way I'm not walking out of here alive."

Stannard clamped a hand on his shoulder. "It's better to die a lawman than as an outlaw."

"I'm no lawman," Nathaniel said, shrugging his hand away.

"You are, if I say you are."

Nathaniel laughed. "Pa wouldn't like that."

Cassidy shook his head. "Brett would like that. He wanted the best for you."

"Even if the best is dying?"

"It depends on what you're dying for,"

Stannard said.

He patted Nathaniel's shoulder before raising his head over the top of the cart. A cascade of gunfire ripped out making him duck down.

"There are ten, maybe twelve gunmen out there," he said. "They're lying down and they've fanned out across the main drag. I'm guessing they aren't good shots or they'd have hit us already."

"What are your orders?" Cassidy asked.

"Keep it simple and move fast, and we might live through this." Stannard pointed at them both. "You'll both move on the count of five. Cassidy, come out on the left. Nathaniel, come out on the right. Shoot at anybody who's close and head for the bank."

Nathaniel sighed. "I guess I didn't want to shoot either of you back there. I know what my pa did was wrong."

Stannard nodded. "I know. Now concentrate on surviving the next few minutes."

While Stannard checked his .45, Cassidy shuffled along the ground to the side of the cart. When they were both ready, Stannard counted down on his fingers. On five, Cassidy threw himself from behind the cart.

He hit the ground, rolled onto his stomach and fired three times at the nearest man, who twitched and then collapsed face down in the dirt. Cassidy rolled to his feet and ran, crouched down, for the bank, shooting his gun until he'd discharged all his bullets at the nearest gunfighters.

His final shot hammered lead into the chest of one more man and then his scrabbling run reached the bank. A moment after he'd found cover, Nathaniel leaped through the empty window and then hunkered down.

Cassidy reloaded, but when Stannard didn't follow them, he checked outside. The marshal had gained cover behind the wagon in front of the bank. Four bodies lay sprawled on their backs, while Digby stood with his arms raised on the hardpan.

"Marshal, we can sort this out," Digby called.

"I can't arrest a whole town, Digby, but if your men throw down their guns, we'll talk,"

Stannard said.

"Don't trust him, Marshal," Cassidy said before Digby could reply. "This town has a secret to protect. They won't let us leave."

Cassidy slipped into doorway. Outside, their opponents rose to their feet and grouped together behind Digby. Bainbridge, Granville and Jebediah were there along with six others who had sat in judgment at Cassidy's lynching. Cassidy reckoned the corruption in this town was probably limited to these men.

Digby strode toward Stannard. "Marshal, I'm unarmed. Let's talk this through. There's clearly been a misunderstanding."

"Don't listen to his lies," Cassidy said.

Stannard raised a hand and strode out from behind the wagon.

"What do you propose, Digby?"

Ten yards from the wagon, Digby stopped. "I don't want to talk to an armed man who has shot four of my townsfolk. Let us talk, unarmed man to unarmed man."

After a few moments silence, Stannard nodded. "All right, but we'll do it back here behind the wagon and out of the line of fire of your men."

"Don't do this, Marshal," Cassidy called. "That man tried to lynch me."

Stannard shook his head. "Cassidy, this is my decision to make. As soon as you start following orders, the sooner you'll remember what it takes to be a lawman."

Digby nodded and strode toward Stannard around the side of the wagon while his men shuffled forward as if they were getting ready for action. Once Digby stood in front of Stannard, the lawman placed his .45 on the wagon.

"So how do we sort this out?"

"Let me show you some evidence that'll convince you things aren't what they seem," Digby said.

Moving slowly, Digby slipped his hand into his jacket. Then, with a sudden yank, he drew out a pistol and without warning he fired. As Digby smirked, Stannard crumpled to the ground with a hand clutched to his stomach.

The men behind the wagon took that as

their moment to act and they sprayed the bank with a volley of gunfire. Cassidy threw himself to the floor as the gunfire ripped across the doorway.

"What are we going to do?" Nathaniel asked as the men outside dashed toward the bank.

Cassidy smiled. "What would Brett have done?"

Nathaniel laughed. "He'd sooner try and fail rather than do nothing. So he'd have stormed out of here firing at anyone that moved. He wouldn't have stayed and waited for them to pick us off."

"That sounds like a plan to me."

When Nathaniel nodded, Cassidy dove through the door. He rolled across the boardwalk and then gained his feet. Then he sprayed a line of gunfire across the three nearest men. Beside him, Nathaniel clattered out of the window and fired at the men approaching from the left.

Without time to see if his shots reached their targets, Cassidy ran for the wagon. Beside Stannard's body, Digby was cowering on the ground and with his bullets fired, Cassidy kicked him in the face, knocking him on his back.

Then he leaped for Stannard's .45 on the wagon. He scooped up the gun and threw himself over the wagon. Bullets ripped into the sideboard as he fell, and with the wagon at his back, he landed awkwardly.

With his .45 still pointed down Cassidy tried to gain his feet. He stumbled and when he righted himself, he faced a line of four men. Granville was on the left and Bainbridge was on the right.

Nathaniel was kneeling on the ground beside the wagon, his hand poised with a handful of bullets ready to reload his Peacemaker. As Cassidy stood tall, Bainbridge nodded at him.

"That was some fancy shooting there," he said. "So do you two want to give yourself up or shall we kill you here?"

Cassidy flexed his fingers, deciding he'd at least kill Bainbridge, the card cheat, even if the rest cut him to shreds.

"Go on," Digby shouted. "What are you

waiting for? Shoot them."

"I can't shoot men who aren't threatening me," Bainbridge said.

"They're armed."

With this, Digby kicked Nathaniel's Peacemaker away and with the back of his hand slapped Nathaniel's face. With Nathaniel lying before him, Digby kicked him on the chin, making him cry out and then lie still.

The four men in front of him turned to this fight, so with their attention elsewhere, Cassidy fired at Bainbridge and then dove to his left. Gunfire blasted around his feet as he stumbled toward Nathaniel and Digby.

On the run he barged into them, knocking Digby to the ground. Then he dragged him to his feet and turned Digby around so he faced the three standing men.

"Put your guns down and reach," Cassidy said. "Then we'll head for the cells."

"Three against one aren't good odds," Granville said.

Cassidy shuffled his arm farther around Digby's neck making the mayor gasp and struggle ineffectually with his arms waving wildly.

"That'll be four against one," Bainbridge said, getting to his feet holding his wounded arm.

Cassidy raised his .45 to Digby's head. "Maybe the odds aren't good, but Digby will die first."

Bainbridge laughed. "You won't do anything. Lawmen don't take hostages or kill them."

"I wouldn't bet on it," Cassidy said.

Nathaniel was out cold and even if he came to his senses, he was ten yards away from his gun. So Cassidy pressed his .45 to Digby's head, making the skin buckle around the barrel.

"It looks like we have a stand-off, Cassidy," Bainbridge said.

"So what do you propose?" Cassidy said.

"You'll get nothing, Cassidy," Digby snickered. "Whatever happens here, you don't get to walk away."

"Then tell me one thing. I don't care what was going on here, but did Wishbone know what you were doing?"

"No," Digby said. "He was a good lawman."

"That's all that matters." Cassidy flexed his shoulders. "Now we're backing away. You'll do the same taking one steady pace at a time or I'll shoot your mayor."

Digby trembled in his grip and gulped. "You heard him. Don't take chances or he'll kill me. Back away."

"You yellow-bellied varmint," Bainbridge snarled. Then he fired, slamming his shot into Digby's chest and making him stagger back against Cassidy.

Cassidy swung his .45 in an arc across the men. He started with Bainbridge and ended at Granville, pulsing his trigger-finger rapidly. Returning gunfire tore out, but it all pummeled into Digby's lifeless body making Cassidy stagger back until Digby's weight made him fall to the ground.

The moment he came to rest, he dragged himself out from under Digby's body, but all the men were down. Only Bainbridge had survived the onslaught and his mouth was wide open with shock.

"Take a look at all this carnage because when you cheated me for a nothing pot, you started it," Cassidy said. He smiled. "Now I'm ending it."

He fired, slamming his gunshot between Bainbridge's eyes. The slug cracked his head back and made him crash down on his back. Bainbridge twitched once and then stilled. Cassidy reloaded Stannard's .45.

Then, with his legs planted wide apart, he waited. As it turned out, the few people that strayed from the stores and saloon didn't come close enough to threaten him. So shuffling sideways, he edged toward Nathaniel, who was already stirring and shaking himself.

"We're leaving," Cassidy said.

Nathaniel noted the bodies sprawled around him and gave a resigned nod. Cassidy checked on Stannard, but Digby's pistol had blasted a wide hole in his chest. With a sigh, Cassidy turned from Stannard's body and strode away.

Outside the saloon, he gathered the reins

of the two nearest horses and led them back down the main drag. At the bank, he loaded the moneybags on to their backs.

"How much do you reckon is in them, Cassidy?" Nathaniel asked as he mounted his horse.

"Whatever the amount, it's not worth the number of men who died trying to steal it."

Nathaniel gave an affirmative grunt and then they swung their horses away from the bank and trotted away. They maintained a steady canter through Redemption City while avoiding meeting the eyes of the few people who came outside to line the main drag.

"Where are we going?" Nathaniel asked, as they passed the last building.

"Beaver Ridge, so we can find someone in authority who can finally sort out this mess."

"How do you know I won't attack you on the way and then steal the money and run?"

Cassidy turned to Nathaniel, but the young man laughed, confirming he had been joking.

"I reckon you've been running for too long already. Now you're ready to face up to a new life."

Nathaniel steered his horse closer to him. "I accept what I did was wrong, but how long do you reckon I'll get in jail?"

"It depends on whether you've remembered what Marshal Stannard said. All lawmen finish what they've started and they never abandon their duty."

"I'm no lawman."

"Aren't you?"

They rode on for a few minutes. When the shacks that were dotted around outside Redemption City gave way to open scrubland, Nathaniel nodded.

"I remember Stannard saying that, and I remember you saying you were in my debt. Are you repaying that debt now by suggesting I'd make a decent lawman?"

"No, I'm still in your debt. I just think you'll make a fine lawman. If you finish this job satisfactorily, no one need ever know everything that happened back there."

"If you don't tell anyone what I did, won't

you be lying?" Nathaniel asked. "Because I thought lawmen always remembered their duty and never avoided the truth."

Cassidy laughed and, as the trail back to Beaver Ridge beckoned, he slapped his horse's flank with his hat.

"It sounds like you've already learned the first lesson of being a lawman," he said, as his horse broke into a gallop.

"What's the second lesson?" Nathaniel shouted after him as he hurried on.

Cassidy waited until Nathaniel caught up with him and then smiled.

"There is no second lesson," he said.

THE LAST RIDER FROM HELL

I.J. Parnham

Staked out under the baking heat of the desert sun by Frank Chapel's riders from hell is no way for any man to die. Only someone as resilient as Matt Travis had the courage to endure the heat and the vultures and survive. When finally he manages to escape a gruesome death only one thing is on his mind – revenge.

But his memory has been blasted to oblivion and he is even unsure of his own name. All he knows is that everyone wants him dead!

Justice must be done and Matt will be judge, jury and hangman. First, though, he must face up to the truth of his past and, that accomplished, lead begins to fly.

2nd *in the Cassidy Yates Series*

Also by the same author

Six-shooter Tales
More Six-shooter Tales
Mendosa's Gun-runners
Calloway's Crossing
Incident at Pegasus Heights
Sharpshooter McClure
Bleached Bones in the Dust
The Prairie Man
Search for the Lone Star
Dead by Sundown
Beyond Redemption
Night of the Gunslinger
The Devil's Marshal
Legend of the Dead
Men's Gold
Bullet Catch Showdown
The Mystery of Silver Falls

Printed in Great Britain
by Amazon